ALEHOUSE

PART FOUR

AFFAIRS IN ZURICH

Nigel Heath

This is a work of fiction. Names, characters, business, events and incidents are the products of the author's imagination. Any resemblance to actual persons, living or dead, or actual events is purely coincidental.

Copyright © Nigel Heath 2022
This book is sold subject to the condition that it shall not, by way of trade or otherwise, be lent, resold, hired out, or otherwise circulated without the publisher's prior consent in any form of binding or cover other than that in which it is published and without a similar condition including this condition being imposed on the subsequent publisher.
The moral right of Nigel Heath has been asserted.

ISBN:9798362161156

My grateful thanks in the preparation of Albany House are due to Marc Bessant Design, my wife, Jenny Davis, Mary Watts and Alexandra Bridger for literary support, to artist Maureen Langford for the cover picture and to my walking companion and poet, Peter Gibbs, for his technical support. Peter's poetry anthology, Let The Good Rhymes Roll, is also published on Amazon.

Chapter 1

"Have I got some news for you Alicia," announced wealthy estate agent Royston Randall, as he entered the green and white tiled hallway of their large Victorian house, set in extensive grounds on a wooded hillside overlooking the North Devon town of Draymarket.
"Daddy, Daddy," his three-year-old golden-haired daughter Corina called as she ran out of the drawing room in front of her mother. Putting down his heavy briefcase, Royston
scooped her up and spun her around before setting her down again, feeling a sudden dizziness as he straightened up.
"You know that's not good for your back Royston," his wife Alicia chided him gently. "I know, I know," he replied, brushing the mild rebuke aside as they embraced. "So what's this news that's so special it could not have waited until later?" she asked.
Royston led the way back into the drawing room and collapsed into one of the two heavy leather Chesterfield sofas drawn up on either side of the large open fireplace, with Alicia taking the opposite one and lifting Corina onto her knee.

"I've spent the afternoon talking business with Mark and he's agreed to buy me out as an investment opportunity, provided I remain in post as MD for the next three years, continuing to grow the business, while training a colleague to take my place. So, what do you think of that darling?" Mark Hammond was a highly successful city hedge fund boss, who'd moved to the area and acquired a small estate some five years earlier and had joined the vintage and classic car owners' club of which Royston was the long serving, honorary secretary.

Both having their own private collections, they'd hit it off almost immediately and had been close friends ever since.

Royston, who never considered himself as being particularly wealthy, had grown his business slowly, but steadily over the past seventeen years. From small beginnings in the nearby village of Hampton Green, he'd taken over a rival family agency in Draymarket and had gradually extended his operations until the Royston Randall chain covered the whole of north and south Devon and most of neighbouring Somerset. Royston had always shied away from the quick fix solution of leasing, preferring to acquire the premises of the mostly independent and family own businesses he took over. Consequently, he had now built up a substantial property portfolio and this was what had made his wholly owned company attractive to Mark as an investment.

"How long has all this been brewing and why haven't you told me about it before?" asked Alicia. "To tell you the truth, it's been on my mind for some time, but I didn't want to raise your hopes by telling you about it until it was a done deal," he admitted.

"You're always complaining that you, Anthony and Corina don't see enough of me, so soon you may be complaining that you're seeing too much of me. But no, seriously, I'm looking forward to having more free time and that can start as soon as Willie begins finding his feet." William Weaver was the always smartly dressed and extremely bright young man, who'd joined the firm four years earlier and had been made manager of his first branch, within just a few months, when his boss suddenly up and left. It wasn't long before Willie, as he liked to be called, was managing even larger branches and, as he was single, he was not averse to moving around and filling in when needed.

"To tell you the truth, I feel right now like a huge burden has been lifted from my shoulders. The thought of no longer spending endless hours on the phone, while being driven around the country by Bob is really beginning to appeal."

Bob Smart, the proud owner driver of a classic black Bentley, had become an important part of the Randalls' small circle of family and close friends after he and his wife Annie had moved into Little Oreford Court, in the nearby village of Little Oreford, as chauffer and companion to the elderly owner, known to all in those parts as the indefatigable Charlie Andrews, nee Potter. "How does Bob feel about the prospect of losing his most important client?" asked Alicia, as she began thinking about all the changes that were now suddenly appearing on her horizon.

She knew instinctively that Bob Smart would have known what was brewing because the two had become confidants, which was inevitable, seeing they spent so many hours together and were both classic car enthusiasts. "He's very much in favour because he too is looking forward to spending a lot more time with Annie, when she's not doing her duty manager shifts at The Oreford," said Royston.

It was true that Alicia had often grumbled about the amount of time Royston spent, either out on business, or with his car enthusiast friends, but she was not really sure she wanted a seismic shift in their domestic arrangements. While she had grumbled, she could have got much more involved with his club, as some of the other more gregarious partners had done, but she wasn't in to cars and all the socializing that went with them. This did make her feel slightly guilty at times because she knew Royston would have really appreciated and welcomed her showing more interest. Alicia Randall was mostly perfectly contented in her own company and with devoting much of her time to her eleven-year-old son Anthony and her definitely outgoing daughter, who'd come along years after she'd given up all thoughts of having another baby. She only had one really close friend and that was Corina's Godmother, Corinne Potter, manager of the Oreford Inn and daughter of Charlie. Corinne's twin sister Laura lived next door at Albany House, a former Victorian rectory in Little Oreford, where her husband Ben ran the Old Mill House Visitors' Centre and Craft Workshops, at the far end of the village green. The couple had two grown-up children, Luke, a climate change researcher, and Lottie, who was married to the Oreford Inn's chef Andy Taylor, and worked part- time at Royston Randall's Hampton Green agency, as her mother had done before her. The couple had seven-year-old twins, Jack and Hannah, and also lived in an annex at Little Oreford Court. Their little lives were a continuing source of joy for their great grandmother Charlie, who felt her long life was now complete. For with chauffer Bob and Annie living in an apartment above the stables and her granddaughter Lottie and family living next door, how could it not be? she often asked herself.

As he was home relatively early, Royston read Corina her bedtime stories before coming down for supper, which they normally ate at a solid oak table in their large Victorian kitchen.

"Do you want white wine with your fish?" he asked, after entering the room and having his senses invaded by the tempting smell and sound of the two large salmon steaks sizzling in the pan.

"Or shall I open a bottle of bubbly to celebrate?" he asked.

"Wine will be fine, and seeing it's such a lovely evening, let's eat out on the patio," Alicia suggested.

It was the Tuesday before the summer holidays, so she would be off on the Friday morning to collect Anthony from his private school, some sixty miles away in neighbouring Somerset. Neither of them had wanted their son to go away to school, but his best friend Michael was going and he'd been determined to go with him. As it was, Anthony loved boarding and all the after school and weekend activities open to him and Michael, and although she missed him dreadfully to start with, it did make life far less complicated and free from the endless weekday treks to and from school.

"I'm working in the Draymarket office tomorrow, so I thought I'd leave before lunch so we could walk up to The Lookout with Corina and have a picnic," he said after they'd finished eating and he'd topped up her glass.

"That sounds like a lovely idea," replied Alicia, instantly remembering she'd invited Corinne around for lunch, but would hopefully be able to put if off to the following day. Her husband, it seemed, was wasting no time in taking the first small step away from the world of work. Had she ever really appreciated the huge burden he'd carried on his shoulder, with over seventy branches and three times as many employees under his wing? she asked herself. It was all right for her. She'd simply enjoyed all the benefits from the wealth he'd created and it made her feel a little uncomfortable.

If Royston was now really going to take life easier, then she would embrace his decision, she resolved.

Wandering up to The Lookout was the frequent treat they'd allowed themselves ever since Royston had acquired a finger of woodland behind their property, including a small area of the ridge overlooking Draymarket to the east and out towards the North Devon coast in the west. Obtaining permission for a small wooden pavilion with wide balconies looking out in both directions had not been easy, but he'd won through in the end, owing to the largely temporary nature of the construction.

As it happened, Corinne was able to change their luncheon date, but she'd not sounded her usual relaxed self, Alicia thought as she put down the phone. They'd arranged to lunch around 1.45,pm so that Alicia would have had time to put Corina down for her afternoon nap and, although it was a little early, her daughter obliged by falling asleep almost immediately. But the moment Corinne arrived, Alicia could tell that all was not well.

"What on earth's the matter," she asked, concern writ large in her voice as soon as Corinne had accepted a glass of wine and they'd settled down under the large sun umbrella over the patio table. "It's Jonathan. He's dumped me and I never saw it coming, which was why it was such a huge shock when he broke the news to me on Skype on Monday night," Corinne said flatly.

"But why on earth has he done that? I thought you two were rock solid," said Alicia. "So, did I," said Corinne, tears welling up in her still bright blue eyes.

She'd met Jonathan Meyer four summers earlier when he and his parents had turned up at The Oreford Inn on a grand European tour in search of their roots.

By an amazing coincidence, it had transpired that he was closely related to both Corinne and her sister and to their mother Charlie and she and Alicia had flown out to Jonathan's home in Toronto for a holiday in the fall. While Corinne was already in love with Jonathan, Alicia, for so long rather taken unintentionally for granted by Royston, slipped into a passionate holiday affair with Jonathan's best friend Shaun Morrison. She returned home only to find she was pregnant with Corina, who Royston, thank God, had always believed was his own, while Shaun was never told. Corinne and Jonathan became long distance partners, being in touch by Skype at least four times a week, and spending all their holidays together. It had been an arrangement they had both willingly accepted because, while there was no way Corinne was going to give up her life at The Oreford Inn, he was equally committed to the family law firm in Toronto.

"What on earth was Jonathan's reason for breaking it off with you?" asked Alicia. "It turns out that a new female partner, called Gloria, was taken on by the firm some six months earlier and although he'd done his utmost to resist it, he had eventually become very attracted to her and she to him," said Corinne.

"God you must be feeling awful," Alicia sympathised, "Awful doesn't go anywhere near it, because one minute I felt my life to be complete and the next, there's this huge black hole in it and I'm feeling overwhelmingly depressed, so much so that I'm finding it a struggle to even get out of bed in the morning," she admitted. So how was it left with Jonathan?" asked Alicia, reaching over and recharging her friend's glass. "I was so shocked, I just closed down on him, which I regretted afterwards because I could see he was very upset too," Corinne explained.

"Maybe he'll find she's not actually right for him and get back in touch," Alicia rationalized. "No, the mirror's broken now and can't be mended, but I guess when I'm in a better frame of mind I should write to him suggesting that perhaps, after all we've shared together, we might at least go on being friends."

Alicia wasn't sure that was such a good idea, but kept the thought to herself and changed the subject.

"I don't suppose you really feel much like eating anything," she said. "You're right, but I'll have a go seeing that you've gone to so much trouble," she said, looking at the large Greek salad, covered over by a cling wrap in the centre of the table.

"Anyway, that's quite enough about me so how's Royston?" asked Corinne. Alicia had been all ready to tell her friend about her husband's pending early retirement, but decided this was now definitely not the right moment. "Oh, he's fine, but he's been getting quite a lot of bad headaches lately and is refusing to go to the doctors and get checked out because, whenever I raise the subject, he says he's too busy." It was as if she was choosing something negative to say by way of coming out in sympathy with her friend. "No that's not good, so you must try and persuade him," said Corinne.

Later that afternoon, she sat down behind reception, and wrote an email to Jonathan, apologising for closing down on him and saying it had all come as a terrible shock, which she was sure he would understand. But at the end of the day, she could understand why it had happened and she hoped he would find the happiness he truly deserved.

Chapter 2

All thoughts about doctors went out of the window when Alicia went to bring Anthony home for the summer holidays. They'd tentatively thought of driving down to the coast on either the Saturday or the Sunday, but all their son wanted to do was to help Royston wash and polish a couple of his cars and to spend hours in his bedroom building a complex new Lego model Alicia had given him as a welcome home present.

Royston was back out on the road on the Monday and came home late feeling pretty tired. Luckily Corina was already in bed and, although he'd only been home 'two minutes,' Anthony had gone off to Michael's for a sleepover. They'd just finished supper when the doorbell rang, highly unusual at this time in the evening because they had no close neighbours who might be popping around for some reason or other. "I'll go," said Alicia, heading along the hall to open their large front door. Standing back from the porticoed entrance step, looking quite unsure of herself, was a middle-aged woman, not particularly smartly dressed, and in front of a saloon car that had definitely seen better days, "Can I help you?" Alicia asked, assuming this caller had somehow driven up the wrong drive by mistake, or was lost and seeking directions. "Might I be addressing Alicia Randall?" the woman asked. Alicia felt immediately on her guard. "And who might be enquiring?" she responded, not getting at all a good feeling about this sudden out of the blue encounter.

"I'm sorry, I do apologies for calling on you unannounced and so late in the evening.

My name is Linda Thompson and I have come here to deliver a letter on behalf of my younger sister Theresa Thompson, whom I think, will be better known to you as Tanya Talbot". The shock was so great that Alicia though she was going to faint. "Wait a minute, I'll fetch my husband." Heart thumping, she retreated back along the hallway and into the kitchen. "What's up darling?" asked Royston, immediately taking in the look of shock on Alicia's face. "There's this odd woman at the door saying she's Tanya Talbot's sister and has come to deliver a letter to us!"

Royston also felt his pulse beginning to race as he followed Alicia back to the front door. "Look, what's this all about?" he demanded, feeling his hackles rising. "As I explained to your wife, I'm Theresa, or should I say Tanya's, sister and I have a letter from her begging your forgiveness for the terrible things she did to you both all those years ago,"

Could this really be happening? Alicia thought, as she began reliving the events of that nightmare evening when this jealous psychopathic murderess forced her way into Royston's old bungalow and made them strip naked and make love in front of her at gunpoint. "If you knew where we lived, why didn't she just mail this letter to us?" Royston asked. It seemed a banal sort of question in the circumstances. "That was the thing. We didn't know where you lived, which is why I drove down here from my home in Birmingham and started asking around in the town. I eventually got directions, but not your postal address, which was why I had to deliver the letter myself and why I needed to ring the bell in order to be sure this was the right house." It was a perfectly logical explanation. "Well now you've found us, I think it would be best if you left," he said sharply.

Looking visibly relieved, the woman turned and retrieved a small white envelope from her passenger seat and handed it over to Royston, before getting back into her car and driving slowly away. They walked back into the kitchen in a stunned silence, where he tossed the unopened envelope into their large wastepaper basket, which would double up as a log container come the autumn. "Don't you think we should at least open it?" asked Alicia. "No, she's told us it's an apology, so I don't think I want to have anything more to do with her," he said.

"Yes, but maybe she's been released from that secure psychiatric unit after all these years, or is about to be, and the letter might at least tell us that, because if they are letting her out, then I think I'd want to know for our own security and peace of mind," Alicia persisted. "Well, if you really think we should," said Royston, retrieving the envelope and slowly tearing it open.

Written in a neat hand, the letter was short and to the point. It confirmed, thank goodness, that she was being detained indefinitely at her Majesty's pleasure, but that she wanted them to know that not a day went by when she did not regret the terrible things she'd done to them and to others.

'There were extenuating circumstances in that I had a terrible childhood, raised in a family where both my parents were alcoholics and drug abusers, who would beat my sister and I at the slightest provocation, but I know that can't be even the slightest excuse for my behaviour,' she wrote. 'I have to face the inescapable fact that to do the things that I did, I must be criminally insane at some deep psychological level and can never trust myself, or be trusted, to come back into the real world ever again.

'I write this in the hope that it might finally give you both some closure.' The letter was signed Theresa Thompson.

"That's rich to talk about closure, when all this letter has done is to force us to relive this nightmare all over again when the passing of the years had started helping us to forget," said Royston angrily, again feeling his pulse racing. "We've both had a terrible shock. Why don't you go into the snug to rest and I'll make us a pot of coffee," suggested Alicia, taking command of the situation. "I think I need something much stronger than coffee," Royston retorted, although he knew he didn't really because his head and started throbbing.

Had there really been closure from the terrible happenings of that night? Alicia asked herself while making the coffee. Or after receiving Royston's explanation as to how he'd become involved with this crazy woman, had they simply pushed the whole incident to the back of their minds? It was a common enough scenario; he'd started seeing her while Tanya was still on the scene and she'd turned up at his bungalow unexpectedly to find them about to have supper together.

"I'm sorry, but I don't think I really want anything now," said Royston, after she'd returned with the coffee pot and a plate of his favourite chocolate coated shortbread biscuits. Alicia sat down beside him and reaching out, took his hand in hers and they both thought about the events of that terrible night.

"Talking of closure, do you think we should share this news with Ben?" Alicia asked quietly after a few minutes It was her friend Corinne's brother-in-law Ben Jameson, who having found out about Tanya's past, had turned up, entered the bungalow by a side door and smashed a half empty wine bottle over her head.

"Oh no I don't think so. Don't forget, he had a lot of therapy afterwards to help him get over the trauma and goodness knows how he might react if he was reminded of what happed all over again." Alicia agreed he was right, "But while this has all been a terrible shock, don't you think we should take comfort from the fact that we now know for certain she's never coming out of that secure mental institution? "she said. Royston agreed, but if she didn't mind, he'd go on up to bed because he'd had a long and tiring day. Alicia continued sitting and helped herself to a coffee and one of the biscuits and switched on the television to catch her favourite food programme, but then she heard a crash. "Oh my God, what's happened?" she uttered. Alicia was off the sofa in an instant and running up the stairs. She found

Royston collapsed and unconscious on the floor in their ensuite bathroom with blood seeping from the wound inflicted when he'd hit his head on the side of the bath. "Oh my God! My poor darling," she cried out again, running back into the bedroom to the bedside telephone. The twenty minutes before the paramedics arrived were seared in her memory for ever. Royston was unconscious, but moaning and there was nothing she could do to bring him around. All she could do was to put a pillow under his poor head and dab his wound with some cotton wool balls from the bathroom cabinet and soaked in warm water from the sink.

Corinne was in the middle of helping out with a particularly busy Monday evening restaurant service when Annie Smart, who was doing a shift behind reception, came and found her. "I've got Alicia on the phone and she sounds in a terrible state, so I think you should get over there right away," she said.

"Can you take the order for table five then?" Corinne asked, thrusting the pad and pencil into Annie's hands and hurrying out to reception to pick up the phone. "Oh Corinne. It's Royston, he's collapsed and has been rushed in to the County General, so can you please, please come over and look after Corina so that I can go to him?" she pleaded. "I'm on my way right now," she said, slamming down the receiver.

Alicia was waiting anxiously out on the front porch with Corina in her now aching arms, when Corinne arrived twenty minutes later.

They quickly embraced before Alicia, who already had her car out on the drive, and the key fob in her hand, sped away.

"Let's go back up to your bedroom and read another story, shall we," Corinne suggested to her godchild. "Is daddy going to be all right?" she asked as they climbed the stairs. "I'm sure he is. He's just bumped his head rather badly." The reassurance seemed to satisfy the child, who quickly fell asleep, leaving Corinne free to go and clear up the mess in the bathroom, but although she did her best to think positively, she could not brush aside an overwhelming sense of foreboding.

Chapter 3

Freelance chauffer Bob Smart was engrossed in watching snooker on television when he heard Annie coming in. He glanced at his watch because it was gone ten o'clock and she'd said she'd be home around 9pm. "Sorry I'm late, but I think there's been some kind of emergency at Royston's because Alicia called in a terrible state and Corinne's rushed over there and I had to help out in the restaurant," she explained. "Oh dear. I'm supposed to pick him up to drive over to Somerset at 8.30am so do you think I should call?" he asked. "No, it's a bit late for that. Perhaps you should wait until the morning," she suggested. It was now past 3am back at The Woodlands and Alicia had still not called so Corinne was becoming increasingly worried, but then she heard a car and walked out onto the front step.

The Porsche stopped right in front of the house and was not driven around to the garage, which immediately set alarm bells ringing. Alicia got out and walked slowly towards her. "He's gone," she said, in floods of tears as Corinne embraced her and also started crying, "Oh! my poor Anthony, he's going to be heartbroken when I tell him." They clung to one another sharing their anguish until the sobbing eventually subsided and they walked back into the silent house. "He never regained consciousness, having suffered a massive stroke, or cerebral haemorrhage, and died just after 2am," Alicia explained flatly, breaking into uncontrollable sobbing all over again. Exhausted, the two collapsed onto the twin beds in one of the guest rooms around 4am because there was no way Alicia could bring herself to sleep in her and Royston's bed.

Corinne was woken by the incessant ringing of the telephone and, instantly wide awake, padded down to pick up the phone in the hallway. "Hi it's Bob here, wondering if Royston still wants me to collect him this morning," he asked. "Bob this is Corinne. I have some terrible news. Royston died from a massive stroke in the County General last night," she said. "Oh my God that's terrible. Poor Alicia." He was tempted to question her for details, but then thought better of it because she sounded so upset. "What more can I say other than to pass on our heartfelt sympathy to Alicia and to ask her to let us know if there's absolutely anything Annie and I can possibly do to help at this dreadful time." He rang off and turned to face Annie, who'd just come back into their bedroom, wrapped in a towel from having a shower.

"Oh! this is terrible and to think he was just about to sell the business and have an easier life," she said, suddenly sitting down heavily on the side of the bed in complete shock and disbelief. "Poor Alicia and poor Anthony and Corina. What a terrible tragedy. It's just not fair," Then a thought struck her. "Don't you think you should drive over to Hampton Green and break the news to Heather and Hannah Brooks, who are going to be absolutely devastated," she suggested. "Yes, Annie I think you're right. I'll go as soon as we've had breakfast, although I'm not sure I want any now."

Alicia was sitting up in bed looking pale and tired, her eyes red from all the tears she'd shed, when Corinne returned. "Will you go and see to Corina, who's just woken up, and dress her while I take a shower," she asked. It was if she was now totally drained of all emotion and acting on some automatic pilot.

Alicia disappeared into the guest bathroom, still not able to bring herself to enter her and Royston's room. Corina seemed to have forgotten that her daddy had not been well and was really happy at being dressed by her much-loved godmother so that was one blessing for now at least.

She was sitting in her high chair and busy eating some small pieces of fruit and squares of buttered toast when Alicia entered the kitchen and it was clear she'd been crying again. "When shall I tell Anthony? He's not due back until tomorrow because Michael's parents are taking them to the beach today, so should I allow him just one last day of happiness?" she asked. "Yes, that might not be such a bad idea seeing we're going to have to start notifying people and making arrangements today," Corinne agreed. She'd decided she was going to stay by her friend's side for as long as she was needed. It was as if cold reality had suddenly stolen over her friend, who, sitting down at the central island breakfast bar, drew a pad and paper towards her. "I think we really must break the news to Heather and Hannah first and then they'll be able to notify everyone else in the company," she said, reaching for the phone. "Oh! Alicia we're both devastated and just can't believe it," said Heather. It was clear, even over the phone, that she'd been crying. "Bob called in about half an hour ago and told us and he's still here if you'd like to have a word with him." Alicia said she'd like that. "Oh! Bob, what can I say, you and Royston were so close and have spent so much time together." She could feel the tears welling up again and tried hard not to break down on the phone. It did not help when Bob replied that Royston was probably the kindest and most thoughtful and generous man he'd ever known.

"Amen to that," she heard Hannah say in the background.

Bob handed the phone back to Heather, "Look Alicia, you needn't worry about a thing when it comes to breaking the news to Royston's colleagues, many of whom have been with us for years. And if there's absolutely anything else we can do then please let us know," she said, before Alicia thanked her and rang off.

"I think we should get smashed in Royston's honour tonight," said Heather. "I agree. Life's never going to be quite the same again," replied Hannah.

Alicia and Corinne's day slipped by in a haze of unreality. George Rollings, the reed thin local funeral director, turned up around eleven. He'd served Draymarket and the surrounding area for many years and Alicia had met him a number of times at social gatherings. He exuded professional sympathy and was gentle in his manner, suggesting she might want to take a couple of days to make up her mind about the funeral arrangements. As Royston was such a prominent member of the community, a service at St Andrew's, Parish Church would give everyone the opportunity to pay their respects, he suggested, but of course, it was entirely up to her.

Once back in his office, he called Jackie Benson the no nonsense Editor and Chief Reporter of The Draymarket Gazette. The two had worked in close cooperation for many years. "Jackie, prepare yourself for a bit of a shock. Royston Randall died of a stroke in the County General in the early hours of this morning," he said without waiting for an initial response. "Bloody hell. Tell me you're having me on George!" she exclaimed. "Sadly no. I've just returned from seeing Alicia to begin making some preliminary arrangements," he told her.

"That's terrible. He couldn't have been more than in his early fifties and I didn't know he'd been ill," she said. "He was fifty-one actually and he hadn't been ill, but that didn't stop him having a massive stroke, apparently," he explained. "Oh! my God, I'm still finding it difficult to take this in. We're joint trustees of the Gazette Charitable Trust and, as you know, I've worked with him for years, especially in the earlier days when I was always chasing him for property market stories. That's going to be one of the biggest funerals the town has seen for years," she said, almost as an afterthought, George couldn't help, but agree, "But I guess it would probably be best if you waited until tomorrow before giving Alicia a call," he advised, Jackie said that was OK because the Gazette had already been wrapped up for the week, but had it been a day earlier, then that would have been a different story!

By early afternoon, Alicia had recovered a little more of her composure, but still felt completely numb as if she'd been given some drug that deadened emotions.

"Corinne, I'm beginning to think I was wrong allowing Anthony one final day of happiness because I expect half the town knows about Royston by now and what if someone should call Michael's parents and give them the news?" she pointed out. "I guess that's a good point," Corinne conceded. "But I'm not sure what we do about it, unless you give Michael's mum a call and find out where they are and I drive you over there now to collect him." Suddenly, all Alicia wanted to do was to scoop Anthony up in her arms and hug him, as if trying to reconnect with part of the lovely man she'd just lost. "Yes, that's what we should do as soon as we've made a snack for Corina."

Her daughter had been as good as gold all day, as if she somehow sensed that something unusual was going on. Jane and Colin Smith had left early and taken their son Michael and his best friend across Exmoor to the seaside town of Minehead for a ride on the famous West Somerset steam railway and were now driving back to spend the rest of the day at their holiday caravan on the cliffs overlooking Combe Martin, which was luckily just under an hour away, when her mobile phone rang. "Hi Jane, I can't explain now, but I hope you won't mind if I drive over and collect Anthony, say around teatime," she suggested. "No, of course not Alicia. You know where we are because you've been before and by the time you get over, we'll be back," The very sound of Alicia's voice told her that something was wrong, but she knew far better than to ask any questions. Corinne already had a child seat in the back of her car because it came with the territory of being a doting godmother and once, they were on the road, the child quickly fell asleep, It was a journey Alicia would never forget as she mentally wrestled with just how she was going to break the news to her son. Neither of them spoke on the way because there was really nothing to say and the fact that it was such a perfect summer afternoon only served to heighten their sense of grief and unreality. At last, they drove into the small caravan and camping site, close to a headland, and Alicia climbed out, leaving Corinne in the car with Corina, who was mercifully still asleep. Anthony spotted their arrival almost immediately and came running over, but the moment he was close enough to see his mum's face, with red raw circles around her eyes from lack of sleep and all the tears she'd shed, he stopped dead in his tracks. "Is there somewhere quiet we can go for a few minutes darling?" she asked.

Sensing something was terribly wrong, he took her by the hand and led her to a nearby seat overlooking the sea.

"Has something happened to Daddy?" he asked quietly, once they were seated with her arm around his shoulder.

"Yes, my love, Daddy's gone to be with the angels."

Chapter 4

Jackie Benson was right. Royston's funeral at St Andrew's Parish Church on a glorious early July afternoon, was one of the biggest the town had seen for many years.

Alicia, who no longer had any close family, sat in the first row of pews with Anthony and Corinne. They'd decided that Corina was still too young, so she was at home, with Florence, a trusted child minder. Heather and Hannah, who'd known 'Boss' longer than most everyone else, having enjoyed a close working relationship with him for many years, sat behind them with Bob. He was by himself because Annie had volunteered to remain back at the house to supervise the final preparations for the wake and also keep an eye on Corina.

Heather and Hannah could not make up their minds as to which of them should say a few words, so in the end, they both came up to the lectern together and spoke in turn, "Boss, because that was what we always called him in the early days, and later only in private when the firm started growing, was the dearest, sweetest, kind hearted and most generous man I have ever known," began Heather, even now feeling her tears welling up. "We first visited Hampton Green, it must be some twenty years ago now, while on holiday from London and fell in love with the village, so much so, that we fantasized about jacking in our librarian jobs and finding work locally. So, when we spotted the job vacancy advert in Royston's window, we opened the door and went in," she explained.

"It was pretty clear he only needed one assistant, but seeing how excited and keen we were, he took us both on and the rest, as they say is history."

It was the perfect cue for Hannah to take over. "Heather spoke of Royston's generosity, so now I will share with you just how generous he was. When Christmas came, he did not just give us a bonus, he virtually gave us half his profit for the past year and that allowed us to go off and travel the world for three weeks between late December and early January."

Now she too began welling up. "When we got back from our travels, we always treated him to a slap-up supper at The Lion and you could tell just how much he enjoyed hearing all about our adventures, which would never have been possible without his generosity."

Sitting together behind them, was the whole Little Oreford Jameson family clan, all with fond memories of Royston.

Laura and Ben Jameson were remembering the afternoon he'd first showed them and their children Luke and Lottie around dear old Albany House, and how Laura, and years later her daughter, had gone on to work part time in Royston's village estate agency. Sitting next to Laura, was her mother Charlie and beside her were Lottie with her husband Andy and their twins Jack and Hannah. Close by, were Charlie's two childhood friends Margo and Robin Lloyd, who'd both taken early retirement and moved back to Little Oreford to live in their parents' cottage beside the green.

Alicia had asked Bob and to give a short reading, followed by another eulogy from Mark Hammond, who spoke of all the tireless years of voluntary work Royston had contributed as secretary of the region's vintage and classic car club.

As he spoke, his eyes wandered towards Alicia, with her long ash blonde hair and slender figure. dressed in black and sitting with her head bowed. Now there was a woman he could definitely fancy, although on his visits to the house to see Royston, she'd always displayed a casual aloofness towards him. Under normal circumstances, Mark would have quickly pulled out of acquiring the Royston Randall estate agency chain as soon as his friend had died. He and Royston had become close, well as close as Mark ever let anyone get to him, and it was in, what was for him, a weak moment that he'd agreed to Royston's suggestion that he and his investors acquire the estate agency. The saving grace had been that Royston would have gone on running the business while training up a competent successor, but now that was not going to be possible. However, overcoming that small difficulty by putting in place a property market experienced General Manager would be a small price to pay for the perfect excuse to stay in touch with Alicia. She would now inherit the ten percent stake which Royston had retained in the agency and might well be in need of a little company once a suitable time had elapsed, he reasoned hopefully.

Jackie, sitting at the back of the church and discreetly taking notes, suddenly had a light-bulb moment idea while listening to Mark, which she resolved to check out with him later.

Alicia had been given the option of holding the wake in the Town Hall, a venue offered unanimously by the Draymarket Town Council, but decided that was far too impersonal.

She decided instead to hold it at home with an open invitation for all to come along, given by the vicar just before the end of the service. Those attending the funeral had been requested not to turn up at the house before 4.30pm in order to give the family and close friends time to return from the nearby crematorium where there was to be a much shorter service.

Mark had called around to deliver his condolences to Alicia several days after his friend's death and had certainly found her more welcoming, or was that just his imagination? He had willingly agreed to her invitation to give a short address on behalf of all Royston's car enthusiast friends.

Anthony had remained sad eyed and completely silent, sitting next to his mum during the service. But with Mark's address and the talk of all the cars that had been such a huge part of his and his dad's lives together, the tears began to flow. Alicia took his hand and held it tight, now fighting to retain her composure which eventually she did. "Anthony, do you want to come with me and Auntie Corinne to the crematorium or would you rather go back to the house?" she whispered as the service was drawing to a close. "I think I'd like to go home now please Mum."

Just before the final hymn, the signal for her to lead her small family out of the church, she turned discreetly to Bob. "Will you take Anthony back to the house please rather than coming on with us?" she whispered.

"Of, course, and I can help Annie entertain Corina and I enjoy doing that," he smiled. Bob was a good man and she would have to make sure that he and Annie stayed really close to her, now there would be no more chauffeuring for him to do, she thought as she walked, head bowed, down the aisle.

Sitting together in the black limousine after the short committal service, Alicia and Corinne began to talk. "You know you spoke of the black hole which opened up for you after Jonathan's call telling you it was all over between you," said Alicia quietly. "Well, I guess I know how you felt now that I have to face the reality that my darling Royston has gone forever. I can't help feeling I rather took him for granted and could have been far more supportive, especially when it came to his beloved motor club. He would have so appreciated that," She was suddenly overwhelmed with regret and started to weep. Corinne reached out and put a supportive arm around her friend's shoulder. "You've had a terrible shock and have been on an emotional roller coaster these past few days, so it's really far too early to start trying to sort out your feelings, especially when it comes to regrets." Alicia thought about this for a moment. "I know you're right, but how do you think you would feel if Jonathan ever called up and said he'd made a terrible mistake?" she asked. "Of course, I've thought about that a lot and the conclusion I've always come to is that I'd say 'no' because I don't think I could bear to risk being hurt like that all over again." Their conversation was cut short as the car came to a crunching halt on the gravel outside the front door.

Alicia had not expected that a great many of the mourners would come back to the house to pay their respects, but she was wrong because Royston Randall with his friendly outgoing personality had gathered a wide range of acquaintances, who all regarded themselves as his friends, during his business life in the town and she and Corinne stood at the door welcoming them for what seemed like ages.

She vaguely recognised most of her guests, especially those who lived and worked in and around the town, but as the flow began to thin, the queue was joined by a lean, athletic and extremely well-dressed man, who had all the tell-tale signs of a business professional. He introduced himself as Richard from the motor club, who'd known Royston for many years.

"I thought I knew all Royston's club friends, but I don't think I've ever seen him before," said Alicia in an aside to Corinne, who'd been rather taken by the stranger. He looked like he'd recently returned from warmer climes,

she thought, deciding she'd seek him out and find out a little more about him, if only for Alicia's benefit.
Draymarket Gazette editor, Jackie Benson, made a point of being among the first to turn up at the house and hovered discreetly in a corner, small plate of food in hand, ready to pounce when Mark Hammond showed up. It was a frustratingly long wait, during which time various towns folk spotted her and shouldered their way through the throng to talk to her, which was annoyingly distracting. But eventually she spotted her prey and neatly intercepted the wealthy man, whom, to her surprise, she suddenly found herself rather fancying. "Mr Hammond, we've never met, but I am the editor of the local paper and I have a small favour to ask," she said, buttonholing him. "Royston and I are trustees of the independent trust which administers the Draymarket Gazette, but following his tragic loss there will now be a vacancy to fill," She paused. "So, I was wondering if I might possibly put your name forward as his successor? We only meet quarterly and I am sure we could all benefit from your wealth of financial business experience."

The proposal, coming out of the blue, certainly interested Mark, so they exchanged business cards and he promised to think about it.

Wine glass in hand and judging that a respectable amount of time had passed, Corinne went in search of Richard and was surprised to find him standing just a little apart from the small group of mostly men, whom she took at once to be Royston's motor club pals. "Hello I'm Alicia's friend Corinne," she said, approaching him with a smile. "I thought I'd come and talk to you because you seem to be on your own," she said, nodding in the direction of the motor club cluster. "Yes, I do feel a little like a fish out of water," he admitted in a surprisingly cultured voice, while returning her smile. "So, have you known Royston long?" She asked. "Oh! we go back a long way. It was he and I who set up the club, when I found myself in Devon for a spell," he replied, looking over at the group, whom Corinne noticed had just been joined by Mark Hammond. "But Alicia said she didn't recognise you," she said casually. "Ah! that's easily explained because I have been out of the country for many years and only found out that Royston had sadly died completely by accident. Oh, but I do hope his widow didn't think I was a gate-crasher and has sent you over to check me out." She could tell by the tone of his voice that he was not being serious, but she still felt her cheeks flushing with embarrassment. "Of course not, because Alicia hasn't had a lot to do with the club and certainly didn't know all his motoring friends. I just saw that you were on your own and thought I'd come over and talk to you," she replied. "Well, I'm very glad that you did because I was beginning to wish I'd never come," he admitted.

"I had fully intended going over and introducing myself to the group as a founder member, but something held me back and it must have been you," he said looking her straight in the eyes.

"You see, had I joined the group, you would never have singled me out for being on my own and that would certainly have been my loss." He was a charmer and she already knew she was attracted to him. "So do you believe in instincts then?" she asked, in a bid to ignore and deflect so obvious a compliment.

"Oh my, yes. I learned long ago to obey my instincts and that's done me some spectacular favours over the years, but of course there have also been a few disasters along the way," he admitted, "I'd love to hear some examples, but I guess I'd better go and see how Alicia is getting along." It was an obvious cue for a date and he picked up on it immediately. "In that case, would you accept an invitation to dine with me? It would have to be tomorrow lunchtime as I have to be back in town tomorrow night." he said. "I'd be delighted and I know just the place. It's called The Oreford Inn and it's not far from here," she replied.

Chapter 5

It was a Tuesday lunchtime in late July and Jonathan Meyer and Shaun Morrison had met for lunch at the revolving restaurant at the top of Toronto's CN Tower. They had a standing reservation for noon on the third Tuesday of every month and it had been a fixture in their diaries for at least five years. The table was always booked for four in case they wished to be accompanied by business guests, but the arrangement was that it would just be the two of them if no confirmation was received the week before. It was here at the same table that in the fall, four years earlier, they had entertained Corinne and Alicia.

Although Jonathan and Shaun were next door neighbours, it had been a month since their last catch up for one work related out of town on business reason or another. "So, how's it all going with Gloria?" Shaun asked as soon as they were seated and had placed their order. "She's subtly pressing to get married and start a family because she says her biological clock is ticking," he replied. "Surely, you're well over due for making an honest woman of her and settling down, aren't you?" he prodded. "Shaun that's being flippant and not very helpful, especially coming from you," Jonathan retorted,

"I did try warning you at the time that taking up with one of your firm's new practice partners, especially one as young, bright and attractive as Gloria, could be just a little unwise, but you wouldn't listen," said Shaun, who was keeping up an uncompromising stance.

"OK I wish I'd listened and not broken it off with Corinne because being separated by three thousand miles of water and only meeting up for holidays did have undoubted advantage," he admitted. "Now whose being flippant?" Shaun replied.

"But if you really don't want to marry her and finally settle down, and it sounds to me like you're having some serious second thoughts, then you must now be up front and honest with her so she knows exactly where she stands. Then at least she can make up her mind and decide what she wants to do. My guess is that if she can't accept the status quo, she'll probably resign and move on, which will let you completely off the hook to reconnect with Corinne, if that's what you really want to do," he said.

"Wise words as ever Shaun, but having dumped her and deeply upset her, I am not sure I have the gall, or the guts, to call her up and say it was all a terrible mistake and can I come back please. Once you've betrayed a woman's trust, can it ever be quite the same again? But putting the boot on the other foot do you ever think about Alicia?" he asked. "Yes, but mostly when I am with one of my regulars and I start imagining it's her," Shaun admitted. "Definitely a case of absence making the heart grow fonder then, but it's a mighty long absence and we were only with her and Corinne for three weeks, at the most," Jonathan reminded him. "Yes, but what a three weeks they were," replied Shaun wistfully. "OK, so I give you a toast," said Jonathan. "To Alicia and Corinne where ever they are and whatever they're doing!"

Back in the UK it was a little after 7pm. All the mourners had finally departed, the motoring group members being the last hangers on, and Alicia and Corinne, both by now physically and emotional worn out, were sitting up the breakfast bar with a pot of coffee. Bob and Anthony were outside giving Bob's beloved Bentley its obligatory after run wash and brush up while Annie was upstairs reading bedtime stories to Corina. Bob would normally have waited until they'd returned to Little Oreford Court but felt cleaning the car might help Anthony take his mind off things.

"You know that chap Richard from the motor club whom you couldn't place Alicia," said Corinne. "I went over and chatted to him and it turns out that it was he and Royston who started the club some thirty years ago." But before she could elaborate any further, Annie joined them having just got Corina off to sleep and all three talked quietly about the day until Bob came in with Anthony and suggested that perhaps it was time they went home. Corinne, who'd earlier decided to stay over because there was no way she was going to leave her friend on her own for at least a couple more nights, went upstairs with Anthony who was now anxious to show her how he was getting on with the complex Lego model she'd given him. She'd already planned to go back to the Oreford Inn the following morning to make sure all was in order, although she knew it would be, and to get ready for her out of the blue lunch date. This was one thing she'd definitely not be sharing with Alicia, at least not for a while. 'I don't even know Richard's surname and he certainly doesn't know I run The Oreford," she said to herself as she drove back though sunlit lanes to Little Oreford the following morning.

She was really looking forward to her date. After all the heartbreak and intensity of the last couple of weeks, the prospect of spending a couple of hours in the company of an attractive and intelligent man, was a most appealing prospect.

All was in satisfactory running order at the coaching inn, as she knew it would be, but she was mildly surprised to find Annie back on reception and suddenly realised that, what with everything else that was going on, she hadn't thought to make any alternative arrangements for her deputy, who from her demeaner yesterday, looked to have taken Royston's death pretty badly. "Oh, Annie, I completely forgot you were on early reception today and that you and Bob must have got home quite late last night," she apologised. "To be honest I'd rather be here taking my mind off things than moping around at home," she said, giving Corinne a reassuring smile. "But how's Bob been taking it all, seeing that he and Royston spent so much time together?" she asked. "Typical man, he's not saying much, although he's the one, apart from Alicia, Anthony and Corina, who's going to miss Royston most of all. But now he's also got something else to think about," she said. "What do you mean Annie?" Corinne asked. "Well, back at Alicia's yesterday, Mark Hammond approached him with the tentative suggestion that, as he was taking over Royston's business, then perhaps Bob might like to consider taking over as his chauffer, because besides keeping an eye on the agency, Mark made numerous commutes up to town. I'm not sure I like the idea because driving Royston around was pretty full on and I think this could mean a whole lot more hours and days away. But that apart, I thought it was well out of order for him to even think of raising it at Royston's wake," she said

"And another thing. I think he's soft on Alicia and I don't think I like that idea either." It was as if some emotional flood gate had opened and Annie was now in full flow. "What makes you think that?" asked Corinne, not sure she liked that prospect either. "It was the way he kept looking at her when everyone was there yesterday. I just happened to look in his direction while going around with the canapes and caught him at it, so I started keeping an eye on him and it was blatantly obvious what he was up to," she confided. "Oh dear, Alicia and I are close, as you know, and I don't think he's her type, but he's wealthy and some would say attractive and, naturally, she is in a vulnerable place at the moment," said Corinne. "That's not all," replied Annie. "According to Bob, Mark was always hanging around at The Woodlands most weekends when he was down and he and Royston would often take one of his motors out for a spin and Anthony would go along for the ride and seemed to quite like Mark," she confided. "Oh dear," said Corinne again, thinking that if Alicia's beloved Anthony, liked Mark then, if getting together with Alicia, was his end game, then he might be in with half a chance. "We must talk about this again later, but right now I need to go and change because I've invited a guest in for lunch at noon. His name is Richard, but I don't intend telling him I'm in charge here, so don't let on if he comes to reception and I'm not around." Annie nodded. 'I wonder what all that's about,' she thought as she watched Corinne walk away. The idea of Mark Hammond and Alicia getting together was definitely not a good one, Corinne mulled over in her mind while taking a shower and getting ready for her date.

There was just something manipulative about him. Perhaps he'd even agreed to acquire Royston's business as a means of staying close to his little family and having the perfect excuse to impose himself on their lives as often as he chose, she speculated, but maybe that was going a bit too far. Of course, easy going Royston, who always saw the best in everyone, would never have seen it that way. So, was she overreacting because, at some level, she didn't want her best friend to have a new partner, because she did not have one? she reasoned. No that was definitely not the case. It was just that she had the unerring feeling that if Mark Hammond wanted something, or someone, then he would move heaven and earth to get it.

How else would he have gotten into the position of being the head of a hedge fund worth multi millions?

Corinne was sitting on one of the benches in front of the inn in the late morning sunshine, catching up on all the local news in the Draymarket Gazette and keeping an eye open for Richard, when she spotted him walking from the direction of their car park. Odd that she never saw him drive by, she mused, but quickly let the thought pass as she got up to greet him.

"Hello again, you are spot-on time," she said, glancing at the church clock, rising up above its cluster of surrounding beech trees on the far side of the green and showing that it was just mid-day. "I'm a stickler for being on time. I'd rather be thirty minutes early than three minutes late," he said closing in on her and holding out a hand which she shook. It was warm and his grip was firm and she liked that. "I've reserved a window table so we'll have a good view of the village green," she said turning and leading the way into the restaurant.

"This is very pleasant and most unexpected I must say," he said, smiling at her when they were both seated. He had a kind open and sun tanned face and was perhaps a little older than she'd first supposed in the dim light of the crowded and noisy reception, and was casually dressed in an open neck cream shirt, smart light brown jacket and matching trousers. "Look I don't even know your name, other than it's Richard," she said returning his smile. "So, I'm Corinne Potter, manager of The Oreford Inn and I live here on the premises," she said, giving up on the idea of not telling him of her role. "No wonder you recommended that we should meet here," he laughed. "Well, let me formally introduce myself. I am Richard Love and I live in Madeira where I'm in the import export business. I happened to be in London seeing clients a couple of days ago when in quiet moment waiting in a hotel foyer between appointments, it suddenly occurred to me to Google the car club to see if it was still running, if you'll pardon the pun, and sure enough it was and there was a note about Royston's passing. We had been pretty close friends all those years ago so, as I had a free day yesterday, I decided on a whim to hire a car through the hotel and drive down for the funeral and now I'm glad I did," he said smiling at her. The obvious reference to her was not lost on Corinne and told her he was interested in her almost as clearly as if he'd said it out loud. Or was he just a natural charmer? she wondered for the second time in less than twenty-four hours.

"You told me earlier that you always believe in following your instincts and that has had some spectacular results," she said, throwing the spotlight back on him.

"That's right, I assume that we all have little voices in our heads that pop up out of the blue now and again and suggest we should do this or do that, well at least I do. Anyway, when they do occur, I mostly always do as they suggest and a typical example might be: 'You haven't spoken to so in so for quite a while so, why don't you give him or her a call?' So I always do and you wouldn't believe the number of times over the years that this has led on to something, mostly in respect of business. And then there have been lots of occasions when the person I am calling has responded with: That's funny I was only thinking of you the other day," said Richard.

"That's happened to me too so do you think we're talking about telepathy?" Corinne suggested. "No, I'm not sure it's that. I think it's more a case of your subconscious suddenly giving you a nudge," he responded.

"It must be lovely living on a sunny holiday island," she said, changing the subject. "I guess so, but I've lived there all my life. You see my great grandfather started the import business and it's been in the family ever since. Like most islands, virtually everything to sustain life from nappies to fuel oil has to be imported from mainland Europe, or elsewhere, so that's what we do. But I was sent back to boarding school in England from aged seven to eighteen and then went on to Cambridge to study economics, so that I would be well prepared to carry on the family firm." There was a pause in the conversation while Lucy, one of their young holiday job waitresses, took their orders. "It seems like your life was pretty much mapped out for you," said Corinne, momentarily thinking back to her own childhood in and out of child care and foster homes.

"Yes, it was, but you see, I didn't mind because there was nothing, I wanted more than to carry on the business." She'd already noticed he was wearing a wedding ring and was wondering how to bring up the subject, but then he spared her the trouble. "But my life hasn't always been plain sailing, especially in recent years, because I lost my wife Isabel from cancer a while ago now. It was a long fight which we lost in the end and because we weren't able to have children, I was left rather high and dry, although I do have a big circle of friends," he told her. "Oh, dear, perhaps this was quite the wrong moment to tell you all that," he said, observing the look of concern on Corinne's face.

"I am so sorry about your wife, but please don't apologise because I had noticed you were wearing a wedding ring and I was beginning to wonder about that," she admitted. "That makes me feel a whole lot better now, so moving on, do tell me how you've come to be running this lovely old coaching inn," he asked. "That is a very long and complicated story, which if I started, we'd still be here at supper time and you've got to be on your way back to London this afternoon, but suffice is to say, this is also an extended family business and I've been here for quite a while now." Richard took the hint and they switched to more general getting to know you subjects, like the sort of music that appealed and their choice of literature, but she did relent a little when lunch was over. "Perhaps we might take a stroll through the village because it would be a shame to leave such a picturesque spot without having a look around and maybe visit the church," he suggested. "Now that is a good idea because my grandfather, the Rev Will Potter, was rector here and my mum spent her childhood in Little Oreford," she told him.

"She's almost eighty now and lives just down the road in Little Oreford Court. My sister Laura and her husband Ben, who have two grown-up children, live in Albany House, the former rectory next to the inn," she said turning and pointing it out. "So, I guess that's where your mum grew up," said Richard. "That's right and Ben runs The Old Mill House Visitors' Centre and Craft Workshops, which is that big building on the far side of the green in front of us," Corinne explained. "I see what you mean about this small village being an extended family affair," said Richard.

They had a quick look inside the centuries old church, refreshingly cool and smelling slightly damp as such old and hallowed buildings often do, before Corinne showed him her grandparents' graves and that of her aunt Cynthia, who had never left home. They all looked neglected in their shady and unkempt corner of the churchyard, which was embarrassing, so she made a mental note to do something about it. The truth was that she probably never would because the Rev Will and Mrs Potter had never been particularly nice to her mother and had practically driven her away after she'd become pregnant with her and Laura.

"I really ought to be going now, but let's spend a few minutes on that shady seat," Richard suggested. It was as if neither of them wanted their chance encounter to come to an end. Instinctively, as they sat down, he stretched out an arm across the back of the old and weathered seat, which would have many fascinating tales to tell if only it could speak. "I know this request is so totally out of order, but would it be so terribly rude of me to ask for a kiss?" Corinne made no reply, but simply turned towards him and their lips met.

It was a long and gentle moment and one which Corinne thought, later, she would never forget. "Now I guess I really must be going, but can I call you after I get back to the hotel tonight?" he asked. "I'd love you to, but I have promised to go back to Alicia's tonight so how about calling me tomorrow evening?" she suggested, briefly reaching out and taking his hand until they'd left the seclusion of the churchyard. This was ridiculous. She was feeling just like an infatuated young girl on her first date.

It was a busy evening at The Oreford and what with one of their regular waitresses on holiday, and another having called in sick, it was all hands to the pump with Annie volunteering to stay on and help out in the restaurant. Thoughts of Richard drifted in and out of her mind as she drove back to Alicia's around nine thirty after the main rush was over. 'Trust me to fall for a guy who lives overseas, but at least Madeira is a whole lot closer than Toronto,' she mused.

Chapter 6

Alicia succumbed to a numbing sense of unreality in the following days after the funeral. Bob turned up towards the end of the week, suggesting that he and Anthony went out to work on valeting the interior of his Bentley before switching their attention to one of Royston's other much prized motors. Alicia came out while work was in progress saying that Michael was on the phone inviting him over for lunch and supper and a sleep over if he wanted. Anthony was reluctant to leave his mum, but Alicia said that was fine by her and Bob volunteered to run him over after he'd hurriedly packed a few overnight things.

Twenty minutes later, she was standing on the steps with Corina watching the Bentley disappearing down the drive. She was just going in when Corinne, who'd popped back to the inn for a couple of hours, turned up and suggested that, seeing it was another sunny day, perhaps it might be nice to make a few sandwiches and take Corina up to The Lookout.

Relaxing on the long bench overlooking a rolling panorama of Devon countryside, dotted with patches of woodland, amid fields of crops, while her godchild busied herself picking daisies, Corinne agonised over whether to tell her friend about Richard and how he'd been back in touch and had invited her out to his home in Madeira. She'd be off in three weeks, having already gone online and booked her flight, so Alicia would have to know sooner rather than later. But before she could speak, it was her friend who raised the subject of men. "So, what am I going to do about Mark Hammond?" she asked.

The out of the blue question came as a shock, especially after she and Annie had been discussing that man. "What do you mean, do about him?" Corinne stalled. "You know he was a regular weekend visitor to the house and that Anthony quite likes him, so I don't suppose it will be too long before he calls up and suggests coming around, probably on the pretence of discussing the business, seeing that I'm inheriting ten per cent of it," she said quietly. "What makes you think it will be a pretence, Alicia?" Corinne questioned. "I just always got the impression he was interested in me, which I just brushed off, not wanting to tell Royston about it for all the obvious reason," she explained. "Then it's easy enough. If you think you could be interested in him, you can be free when he invites himself, over, but on the other hand, if you don't want to encourage him, then just don't be available and he'll soon get the message," she advised. "Yes, but would that be fair on Anthony, seeing that he quite likes him?" Alicia asked. "Oh, he'll soon forget all about Mark if you asked Bob if he'd like to take charge of the car collection with Anthony's help. They'll make a great team and I'm sure he and Annie would love that, seeing they have no family of their own," she suggested. "Corinne that's a brilliant idea, but speaking of Bob, Annie's told me that Mark approached him at the reception and tentatively suggested that he now become his private driver," she said, changing the subject. "Yes, I know, Annie told me that too," Corinne replied. "But she doesn't think Bob would even consider it, seeing he's already talking of winding down and taking life a bit easier, so if you do invite him to take charge of Royston's collection, then I'm sure Anthony would, soon forget all about Mark." Corinne got up and went and sat on the grass to help Corina make her daisy chain.

Deep in thought, Alicia began repacking their picnic basket as she watched them. So did she really want to cut Mark out of her life when there were no other companiable men on the horizon?" she asked herself. Yes, she had found his subtle attention embarrassing, especially with Royston being completely unaware of it, but was that enough to rub him out of their lives? After all, he'd been a good friend to Royston, even agreeing to acquire his business, so that her hard-pressed husband would have a chance to retire and take life a whole lot easier. So, what was she to do about Mark, since making a deliberate point of snubbing him was just not in her nature. Anyway, there was really no need to think about it anymore for the moment, she decided.

While threading their way back down through the beech woodlands to the house, she told Corinne she was not sure how she felt about Mark and would just have to take one thing at a time with her emotions being so all over the place at the moment. It wasn't exactly what Corinne wanted to hear because she was feeling particularly protective over her best friend, but It was Alicia's life and whatever she decided to do in the longer term would be OK with her. Besides, who was she to be the judge over what was right, seeing she'd just booked to go and stay with a man she'd actually only known for just a few short hours and on the strength of a single kiss!

Corinne stayed for a cuppa, while saying she really should be getting back to Little Oreford to help out with the evening restaurant service as they were still short staffed.

But over tea she did tell Alicia all about Richard and her friend was so enthusiastic and pleased for her that she really wondered why she'd made such a drama out of it. Funnily enough, after she'd gone and Alicia had bathed Corina, read her to sleep with a couple of stories and come downstairs to a house that was now completely empty, she surprised herself by feeling strangely liberated with only herself to think about for the first time in many years.

Relaxing out on the terrace with a large glass of good white wine, she began taking stock of her life and, after the second generous refill, found herself beginning to look at things from a new and completely unexpected perspective.

Royston had been a wonderful, loving and generous man and she'd always been tremendously fond of him. But she had never really loved him, at least not in the way she'd fallen head over heels for Shaun on their three unforgettable weeks with him and Jonathan in Toronto. She'd returned home, pregnant with Corina, or at least all her instincts had told her she was his child and had then inwardly pined for him for months on end in the quiet moments of her life.

"I wonder what those boys are up to now and whether I should try and find out," she said aloud to herself, but then realised this was probably not the time, seeing that Corinne had been so in love with Jonathan before he'd dumped her and was now on the brink of falling in love all over again. Suddenly she felt an overwhelming tiredness and took herself off to bed, not in the spare bedroom, where she'd slept since the terrible night of Royston's death, but in their marital bed.

Within a few moments she was overcome with grief and began weeping all over again. 'What an emotional mess I'm in,' were her last thoughts before sleep mercifully overtook her.

When Corinne got back to The Oreford, it suddenly occurred to her to check the hotel diary, which, what with everything else that had been going on, she hadn't looked at for a couple of days and it was just as well she did. For at noon the following day, she saw she had a luncheon appointment with a Michael Silver, who now headed up the County Community College's catering and hospitality department. He'd invited her to dine in their Concepts Restaurant, which was open to the general public, and was where his catering students showcased their culinary and front of house skills. The luncheon appointment had been arranged by The Oreford's inspirational Head Chef Andy, who'd first come to work at the inn some years earlier and had fallen in love and married her sister Laura's daughter Lottie. The couple and their twins, lived in an annex at her grandmother Charlie's home, nearby Little Oreford Court. The reason for the luncheon was because Michael Silver had earlier contacted The Oreford to see if the inn would be prepared to offer work experience placements to some of his students. Corinne had opened the initial letter, but had passed it straight on to Andy because that was his department and he had jumped at the idea. After all, the former chef at The Oreford had taken him on when he'd arrived fresh out of college, so now here was the perfect opportunity to repay that kindness. The county college campus stood in its own grounds, a thirty-minute drive away up the North Devon link road towards Tiverton and students there were poised to break up for the summer.

Luckily, there were still enough of them around to direct her to the Catering Department and its smart Concepts Restaurant where Michael was waiting to meet her. She judged him to be around forty, slim, smartly dressed in a light brown jacket and matching trousers, and with an outgoing personality and easy charm, not altogether unlike Richard's and her ex, Jonathan.

Suddenly thinking of him, even though she was shortly to jet off to Madeira to stay with Richard, still gave her a pang of loss. "Believe it or not, your work placement request fits rather neatly in with our whole ethos of encouraging local young people to consider a career in catering and hospitality," she told him, after they were both seated and a visibly nervous white jacketed young student waiter had taken their order. "I am delighted to hear that, but do elaborate," he invited. Corinne told how she and her sister Laura and her brother-in-law Ben had been given access to a substantial sum from their family trust fund to invest for their future now, rather than later. "So we decided to acquire a number of older Victorian properties in the area around Little Oreford and to establish them as satellite holiday guest houses to feed customers into our Oreford Inn for lunch and dinner, if you'll pardon the pun. The aim was also to drum up holiday visitor business for the village's Old Mill House Visitors Centre and Craft Workshops, which we also operate. and this has proved to be most successful," she explained. "What a clever idea I must say, but how does this work when it comes to encouraging young people to take up careers in the hospitality and catering industry?" Michael asked.

"It works because, by and by, we found we were employing more and more local young people to run the guest houses, who were not going on to higher

education. So, my brother-in-law Ben, suggested it might be a good idea to support anyone who was interested in the opportunity of taking day release courses in hospitality, catering and hotel management," she said.
"What a splendid idea, so are they coming to us?" Michael asked enthusiastically. "Well actually no," replied Corinne, feeling herself flushing with embarrassment. "You see, Andy trained at your rival college, just over the border in Somerset, so they go there for their courses. But they've never asked us to provide work placements, while you have so that's why we are going with you," she explained. "Well, that's good then and I can't tell you just how much we do appreciate it because, believe it or not, it's often quite difficult finding enough places willing to accept catering student," he explained. "I guess I can understand that because it's not always easy watching over students in a busy kitchen where everyone's working under a great deal of pressure," said Corinne. "That being the case, it makes your offer of help even more appreciated, but let's stop talking shop and might I ask you to tell me something about yourself and how you come to be managing The Oreford Inn?" he said, neatly changing the subject, "That's a very long and quite complicated story and it would take ages to tell," she replied, suddenly having the

weirdest of deja vous feeling that she'd been here before, namely with Richard on the afternoon following Royston's funeral. "So, what about you?" she countered, swiftly turning the tables on him.

"Luckily my story is comparatively straight forward and I can give you the gist of it in a few minutes," he said, smiling directly at her which was just a little unnerving. She was quite taken with Michael Silver, she'd decided. "I always wanted to be a chef from quite an early age so, against my parents' wishes because they thought I could do much better, I got a job as a sixteen-year-old pot washer at one of the big London hotels. Luckily for me, our Executive Chef was a truly inspirational professional, who once he saw I was keen and willing to work hard, did everything he could to encourage my career. The result was, that over the next five years I progressed through the ranks, while studying part time for all my catering qualifications along the way. But I had only been made up to Sous Chef a couple of months when he took early retirement and, once he'd gone, I really felt it was time for a change. So I went to work at a country house hotel in The Cotswolds for a couple of years before moving on to another one in neighbouring rural Warwickshire, where I took over as Head Chef for the first time." He paused to take up a linen table napkin and wipe his mouth, and she noticed he wasn't wearing a wedding ring. She was also impressed that the college restaurant could afford the linen, but kept that to herself. "So what happen next because, according to my watch, you are still inside the few minutes zone," she joked. "After a couple of years there, I happened to run into a colleague from my London hotel days, who was working on cruise liners in the Caribbean and said it was hard work, but thoroughly enjoyable and I was instantly attracted to the idea and the rest as they often say is history," he told her.

"Well not quiet because you haven't exactly finished the story," Corinne said. "But I must have run out of time by now," he pointed out. "Yes. you have, but I'm giving you a limited extension," she smiled, taking an exaggerated look at her wrist watch. "OK I was at sea for a further five years working for various cruise lines around the world before coming ashore to take over here. So now you know all about me and I know absolutely nothing about you which really isn't fair is it?"

Corinne replied that it wasn't and gave him a brief potted history of her family life before they returned to discussing his student work experience placements at The Oreford.

They had been chatting for over an hour and had just finished coffee when Michael said she would have to excuse him because he had a staff end of term briefing meeting starting shortly. "But look, would you like to meet up for dinner one evening next week because I have so enjoyed our hour together?" Corinne, taken completely by surprise by the unexpected invitation, said 'that would be nice' and taking a business card from her bag, suggested he might call her in a couple of days to fix a date.

'What have I just done?' she asked herself as she drove away from the college, knowing she'd arranged to Skype Richard in Funchal at 9pm. She was strongly attracted to him and was looking forward to her out of the blue holiday, but there again Michael seemed a really nice chap, so what would be the harm in spending an evening with him? After all she was a completely free agent now that Jonathan had dumped her.

Chapter 7

Mark Hammond's private executive jet had just reached its cruising altitude and was enroute for Zurich where he was to chair a meeting of his international investors the following morning. His smart suited personal assistant, Adele Addison, was seated towards the rear of the cabin where she was just putting the finishing touches to the agenda they had discussed earlier. She was a long experienced and highly qualified accountant with an up to the minute, and at her finger tips, knowledge of the world's often turbulent financial markets. She was a single woman and worth her weight in gold, which was why Mr Hammond, she only ever called him that, paid her a cool one million dollars a year for her services.
It was on occasions like these that Mark allowed himself the luxury of taking stock of his life and of all his achievements over a large gin and tonic while waiting for his private chef to prepare and serve him a light supper. He'd been down on his North Devon estate a couple of days earlier where he had summoned in and made Royston's nominated successor, William Weaver, Chief Executive of the Royston Randall estate agency chain. He'd been impressed by the young man's easy charm and sharp intellect and had promised him a substantial

bonus if the agency continued to perform above expectation and 'no' he would have no objection if Willie wished to continue his former boss's expansion plans to cover the whole of Somerset.

Mark Hammond was a man of many appetites and had suddenly found himself resisting an urge to come on to the young man, whom he'd gained the distinct impression was gay.

However, right now, it was the fair, quietly spoken and understated Alicia Randall, who was in his sights and he had long ago started fantasizing about having his way with her.

She was definitely not the most attractive woman in the world, but there was something about her looks and her quiet manner that definitely turned him on. But there was no hurry and he would bide his time before inviting himself over to talk about the estate agency business and his decision to appoint William Weaver to run it. He'd also decided to take up Jackie Benson's invitation to replace Royston as a trustee of The Draymarket Gazette, which could only serve to further integrate him into the local community. Yes, Mark was, according to his own lights and the opinion of many of his colleagues and investors, an extremely astute operator, who without doubt, had been remarkably successful in his business life and yet he was only forty-five, so who could tell to what further heights he might aspire over the next twenty years.

Yet to start with, his was not a particularly remarkable story.

Raised as an only child by working parents, both teachers at a comprehensive School in Kent, he'd studied economics at Cambridge and had gone on to join an investment bank before becoming a market trader, where a natural flare combined with an uncanny knack of knowing just when to take a calculated risk, he had quickly become the highest paid member of the team.

Over the next four years, he amassed a considerable fortune, but nowhere near enough to launch the hedge fund, which was his end game, so how to acquire the additional funds, now that was the question.

It was at times like these, and there had been a couple of them along life's highway, that he had chosen to bide his time and wait for a solution to materialise and on this occasion, it had come from a most unexpected quarter and as a result of a surprise invitation.

Mark had acquired few friends among his colleagues along the way. They were his rivals, and therefore competitors, and he had no wish to spend more than the minimum amount of time with them, beyond that which was acceptable to being recognised as a team player. However, there was one exception and he was Jamie Mackeson, whom he'd met at Cambridge and was now well on his way to making his own personal fortune brokering high-end city property deals. It so happened that Jamie had arranged to fly five prospective clients out to the Dominican Republic in the Caribbean for five days at an exclusive beach resort, golf and country club and one had pulled out practically at the last minute, so he had suddenly thought of Mark.

"I seem to remember you telling me you played a lot of golf in your younger days Mark," he reminded him.

"That's right, but I haven't picked up a club in years so what are you proposing Jamie?" His friend had called around 7pm when, he'd just come off the phone from a close contact in Singapore. Under normal circumstances, Mark would never have countenanced taking off at such short notice, but suddenly his instincts told him to accept. Four evenings later, he was enjoying a quiet drink by himself overlooking the ocean. Jamie and the other members of the group had gone in to dinner, but Mark had had quite enough of their enforced company for one day, so had excused himself.

"Do you mind if I sit here?"

The voice was cultured and undoubtedly Spanish. Mark turned in his chair to find a well-dressed man, whom he judged to be in his early fifties, hovering uncertainly over the only other empty table occupying this particular corner of the hotel lounge balcony.

"No not at all," said Mark smiling. "Do be my guest." His neighbour eased himself slowly into a chair, as a white coated waiter materialized by his side, and he ordered a single malt whisky, which he requested be served in a glass tumbler with two cubes of ice. "Might I offer you drink Senor?" he asked.

Normally Mark would have politely declined, but he'd almost finished his gin and tonic and there was just something about this fellow guest that intrigued him. He seemed to be possessed of a certain old-world charm and was clearly wanting to start a conversation. Mark accepted the invitation and formally introduced himself as a London market trader enjoying a short golfing break with a friend and his guests, "It is indeed a pleasure to make your acquaintance Mark. I am Edelmira Sanchez and I am here for a meeting with my son-in-law, who is due to fly in, from San Jose, Costa Rica, tomorrow morning. He was supposed to have arrived this afternoon, but some last-minute business has delayed him."

Over the next two hours, the first spent on the balcony and the second in the restaurant where they had adjourned for a light super, Mark learned that his fellow guest headed up the Jimarenal Corporation, a business enterprise with significant interests throughout the Caribbean and Central and South America.

It also controlled a world-wide luxury resort hotel chain which had been built up over recent years by his son-in-law and daughter, Francesca.

"So, Mark as an experienced, and from what I can see, a highly successful market trader, what would be your advice if we were looking to withdraw substantial funds from our Latin American operations and reinvest them in the city of London? This, you will understand, is purely a hypothetical question." Was this really happening?' Mark asked himself. He drew a deep breath to calm a heart that had already started beating faster at the prospect of acquiring a new investor, possibly one with enough cash to enable him to launch his long-desired hedge fund!

By now Edelmira had completely won him over with his combination of gentle fatherly interest and completely understated charm and before he knew it, Mark had stepped right out of his stand-offish cards close to chest comfort zone, and had set out his whole hedge fund creation strategy.

"It seems to me Mark that our chance meeting was a moment of great good fortune for both of us," said Edelmira softly as he quietly drummed his fingers on the glass topped table, while peering into the middle distance. This eager young man, so reminded him of that first occasion, he'd met his future son-in-law Brad Meyer in the Panama City airport lounge.

It was agreed that, subject to his son-in-law's approval, and that of the board of directors and with a rigorous regime of checks and balances, the Jimarenal Corporation would transfer forty million US Dollars to Mark's newly created fund.

Back out on the golf course the following morning with a warm breeze drifting in from the ocean, the game was interrupted by the sound of a private helicopter flying in low to land on the pad next to the hotel.

'Here comes the answer to all my prayers,' thought Mark, looking up, golf driving wood in hand, but, of course, he kept that thought all to himself

A sudden small change in the engine note of his private jet, brought Mark out of his self-congratulatory musings and coincided with the arrival of his specially prepared in-flight supper. At first, his dealings with the Jimarenal Corporation had been rather a pain because, despite their initial assurance that they would give him a completely free hand, they'd insisted on signing off on every significant deal, but that subsided once he'd gained their complete confidence. Then five years ago, and quite out of the blue, they'd withdrawn all their now substantially increased funds, but by that time his operation had grown so large, he hardly felt the loss. 'Still meeting up with Edelmira Sanchez all those years ago, had indeed been a remarkable stroke of luck. But that was all in the past and now he was looking to the future and, if he was successful in his campaign, then to the delicious prospect of slowly undressing one, in his eyes, beautiful widow, Alicia Randall!

Chapter 8

It had already been a long morning for Corinne Potter. She'd left home at five am for the two and a half hour drive along the North Devon link road to Tiverton, up the M5 and then off on the A38 through the Mendip Hills to Bristol Airport. She was now safely strapped in to her window seat on a packed charter flight bound for the sunny Portuguese holiday island of Madeira.
Richard had advised her to book a window seat because Funchal Airport was right on the edge of the island, just north of the capital, and close to the hillside, so the views coming in could be spectacular, if not a little thrilling, especially as aircraft had to jam on their brakes as soon as they landed to avoid running off the end of the runway and into the ocean. Corinne, whose entire flying experience had only been on half-a-dozen, long-haul jet flights to Toronto to see Jonathan with the later exception of their trip to Costa Rica, was not at all sure she did 'thrilling,' especially on an aircraft as jam packed as this one appeared to be.
Still, she now had the luxury of three and a half hours of free time to sit back and think because the last few weeks following Royston's death had passed in an absolute whirl of activity, not to mention her frequent late

evening Skypes with Richard, which tended to drift on into the early hours, leaving her tired when she woke to yet another busy day.

Their conversations had covered the whole range through books, music, history, international politics, with the inexorable rise of China, and the state of the poor old planet with climate change looming. Richard was widely read and had his own view on most topics because, not having a partner and living on a small island, what else was a chap to do?

There were only so many evenings one could spend dining or socialising with friends, he joked. But there was one topic Corinne insisted she did not wish to discuss under any circumstances and that was Madeira itself because she wanted it all to be completely fresh experience. She knew the island was mountainous, had a temperate climate and exported wine and bananas, but that was the extent of her knowledge. She'd even gone to the point of not wanting to know anything about Richard's home, which he thought was perhaps a little excessive, but if that was what she wanted, then that was OK with him.

And then Corinne had her slowly developing relationship with Michael Silver to think about and that put her in a bit of a bind because while he was clearly interested in her, she saw him more as a friend and she'd need to make that clear to him before things went much further. She'd meant to do it last week when they'd met for supper at The Cheringford Arms, but something held her back and that, she felt, had been a mistake, especially as she was now on her way to Madeira to be with Richard.

Still, she'd never been to Cheringford before and the first thing that struck her was just how like Little Oreford it was, apart from the fact that it had a centuries old stone bridge at its heart and a ford close by where the river could still be crossed by a four-by-four in the summer. The Cheringford Arms had also been a yesteryear coaching inn and was not entirely unlike The Oreford. But there the similarities ended because it was clearly run down and tired and was crying out for attention, although it still retained a certain quaint old-world charm which was what Michael had said he liked about the place.

While Corinne was chatting with Michael, she was at the same time envisaging what an injection of cash could do and whether the place was privately owned and freehold. "Have you been coming here for a long time?" she'd asked casualty. "I've known the Landlord Jim and his wife Lizzy for a couple of years, ever since their son was a student of mine and now, he's running the kitchen here, a bit like your nephew Andy," he replied.

If the couple had been running the inn for many years, and they owned the property, then, they just might be ready to sell up and if so, this would make a great investment for the Jameson family trust fund, she mused. "A penny for your thoughts, Michael had asked, bringing her daydream to a sudden end, but she'd decided to keep these possibilities to herself, for the time being anyway.

When the holiday jet came in to land at Funchal, Corinne was relieved to see that her window seat was on the side of the aircraft away from the cliff and looking out over the open ocean, still the aircraft seemed to be swaying about in the wind and that was quite enough excitement for her. Collecting her luggage from the carousel, she made her way out into the arrivals hall and quickly spotted Richard in open neck cream shirt and casual matching shorts waiting to greet her. She came forward, small travelling suitcase in hand, and they hugged, which seemed to both to be the most natural response, seeing that while they'd chatted together for hours and hours, they'd only ever shared one brief, albeit. quite passionate kiss. "Well, here you are," he said smiling as they stepped apart. "Yes, here I am," Corinne replied happily.

"So now we'll go home, so you can freshen up and take it easy after your journey, but first I thought we'd take a drive along, what you would no doubt call the prom, so you can get your bearings," he suggested. He led her out into the warm midday sunshine and into a packed carpark where he made towards a large open topped jeep with the name Maisy emblazoned on the side, hand written in bright yellow paint. "And this is my other girlfriend," he announced. "I'm delighted to meet you Maisy," she said, catching his mood, as he took her case and placed it on the back seat before opening the passenger door for her to climb in beside him. With a growl, the powerful diesel engine roared into life and they were soon speeding along the coastal highway with the city opening up on the sloping hillside in front of them, but she was slightly disappointed at just how built up it appeared to be.

"Rather than driving, do you think we could park up and go for a walk because it seems like I've been sitting down for hours and hours and I could do with stretching my legs?" asked Corinne.

Five minutes later, they were strolling, hand in hand, through the crowds of tourists along the tree lined promenade with several giant cruise ships docked at the ocean terminal filling the skyline in front of them. Corinne was feeling absurdly like a teenager out on her first date with the delicious prospect of all that lay ahead. "Is that a cable car station over there and if so, where does it go?" She asked. "It ascends to Madeira's famous botanical and Monte Palace Gardens and there are amazing views out over the city and the ocean on the way up, so we really must do it before you go home," said Richard. Twenty minutes later, they were back in Maisy and winding their way up through a warren of narrow streets clinging to the hillside. Before she knew it, they were swinging in through a pair of wrought iron gates set, in a high wall, to enter a large tropical garden with an old colonial style two-storey house with heavy green shutters set at its centre.

"Goodness Richard if this is your home, it's amazing!" she exclaimed. "Yes, this is my oasis of calm in what, over the past thirty years, has become a pretty busy port city with thousands of tourists either jetting in or coming ashore from the cruise ships all the year around and, to tell you the truth, I find it all pretty frenetic and relentless at times," he admitted, "Still the busier it gets, the more people need to consume and the more imports are needed and that's how I make my money, so I definitely can't have it both ways," he laughed. "Do you want to go inside or shall I show you around my garden first?" he asked. "Oh! let's do your wonderful garden first shall we?"

Corinne had never had any time in her life for gardening, other than to make sure the The Oreford had a magnificent show of bright red geraniums in its hanging baskets all summer long, but felt it was a hobby she might take up one day.

Strolling around sunlit gravel paths, partly shaded by exotic looking trees, Richard took great pride in pointing out some of the rarest, and to him most interesting, plants and flowering shrubs, among the hundreds to be seen all around them.

Turning a corner, they came upon a large lily-filled pond with a magnificent life-sized bronze of a nude young woman sitting at the far end, leaning over and washing her long hair in the water.

In an instant, Corinne was on the patio with Jonathan in Toronto watching Alicia slowly stripping naked to go for a cooling dip with Shaun, what now seemed like a lifetime ago. Suddenly a small cloud of doubt about what she was now doing, drifted into her mind. "She is rather magnificent, isn't she?" said Richard.

"She certainly is, but she looks a bit lonely, so shouldn't

she have a male companion at the other end, perhaps, with a fig leaf to preserve his modesty, don't you think?" she replied, tearing herself back to her present reality. "That is a thought, but maybe not with the fig leaf. After all, if she is as nature intended, surely he should be too." Now they were standing side by side gazing at the young woman and suddenly his arm was around her shoulder and, as if to banish all thoughts of Jonathan, she slipped hers around his waist and slightly up under his loosely hanging shirt, so that her fingers slowly connected with his warm, smooth body. It was a brief moment of intimacy.

"Now I must show you one of the most magnificent private views over the city," said Richard, leading her along a path towards a railing. It was only now she realised the garden was perched on the edge of an escarpment with, as he had promised, the most sensational view. "Are you ready for some lunch?" he asked after they had stood together gazing out for a couple of minutes and he had pointed out some of Funchal's landmarks.

"I am beginning to feel a little peckish," she admitted, thinking back to the rather small sandwich she'd eaten on the flight out, together with a packet of crisps and washed down with a tepid cup of quite disgusting coffee dispensed from a large silver pot.

"I have asked Francis to prepare something light because I thought you might want to take a nap afterwards, as I'd like to take you out for an early supper beside the ocean this evening," Richard said, leading the way back towards the house.

"And who is Francis might I ask?" she replied. "Putting it bluntly, he's my personal aid, whose is in charge of the house and all my domestic arrangements and looks after me rather well I might say," he explained. "You mean a bit like a Jeeves," she said.

"Yes, a bit like that, but I can assure you that I'm certainly no Bertie Wooster," he joked.

As they walked past the jeep, she noticed her luggage was no longer on the back seat and had now been deposited in the airy terracotta tiled hallway, they'd just entered. "I thought I'd give you the grand tour later," said Richard, leading the way into a large kitchen where a tall thin man in an apron was standing poised with a tray of food, ready to be taken out through open double doors onto the patio beyond. "Francis, this is Corinne," Richard announced. "I am very pleased to meet you, but you'll pardon me if I don't shake hands, only mine are otherwise engaged at the moment," he smiled broadly.

As they followed him outside, her thoughts flashed back to that evening in Toronto when she and Alicia had been introduced to Shaun's handyman and gardener Lewis, as the giant of a man was busy cooking steaks on his poolside barbecue. Again, she thought of Jonathan and was possessed of a sadness.

Now seated opposite one another, she and Richard helped themselves to a huge Greek salad. "I apologise for this not being a traditional local dish, but I am very partial to Greek salads and at least the bread is freshly baked," he pointed out.

"I love Greek salads too, but now tell me all about Francis," she invited. "There's not really a lot to tell actually." He was a Head Waiter on one of the big cruise ships, whom I met in a bar one evening when he was in port. We got to talking and he said he was looking for a way out and, on the spur of the moment, I asked him if he'd like to come ashore and work for me and he jumped at the idea. That was a few years ago and since then he's married a local girl and the couple have one of the many gift boutiques at the bottom of the town. They live in an apartment over the shop and while she manages the business, Francis walks up the hill every morning to helps me," he explained, "It sounds like the perfect arrangement all round," she said.

After lunch, he took her on the promised grand tour of the house which got no further than the guest bedroom. Corinne saw at once that an unseen hand had deposited her luggage at the foot of the large double bed. "I thought you might want to take a short rest," he suggested as he stood by her side. "I think perhaps we might leave resting until just a little later she said turning towards him, placing both arms around his neck and kissing him gently full on the mouth for only the second time in their relationship. It was as if she was again trying to exorcise Jonathan from her thoughts.

"How could I possibly argue with that suggestion," he said, now pushing the bedroom door quietly shut behind them with a foot and leading her back towards the bed where they slowly undressed one another between kisses. After all there was no hurry!

That evening, as promised, he took her out to one of the small restaurants in the old colonial part of town where they dined on tuna steaks with fried maize

At some point during the evening, he began talking about his late wife Isobel, whom he'd met at an import-export trade conference in London. "To tell you the truth, the five short years we shared together were the happiest of my entire life. She worked as the personal assistant to the managing director of a London based general goods export company and had various short-lived affairs along the way. That was probably because of her fiery temperate and, quite honestly, she could be outrageous at times. But the great love of her life was her oil painting, which she said, always calmed her temperament. I invited her out to Funchal and she quickly fell in love with the island because of its sheer vibrancy and spectacularly high mountains and deep valleys and decided it would be the perfect place to settle down and paint. We married shortly afterwards and started trying for a baby, but it simply didn't happen for us and then five years later she was diagnosed with breast cancer, but the disease had already spread and she sadly died six months later." Now there were tears in his eyes. "Oh, Richard how terribly dreadful," she said reaching out and putting the palm of her hand over one of his wrists. "Now tell me about your past relationships," he invited.

This was the moment Corinne had been delaying and had purposely avoided during all their laten night chats, but now there was really no way out of it. "There's not really much to tell actually. I met a Canadian called Jonathan some years ago when he came with his parents to stay at The Oreford and a few months later

Alicia and I flew out to Toronto to spend a short holiday with him. She paused to take a sip of wine.

"Well one thing led to another, as it generally does, and I fell in love with him with the result that we embarked on a long-distance relationship. He was the head of his family law firm and totally committed to it, as I was similarly committed to The Oreford, so we did what we have been doing, keeping in regular touch by Skype and having holidays together three or four times a year. But sadly, he fell for one of his firm's new business partners called Gloria and dumped me," she explained.

"I guess I am anchored to my business in much the same way that your ex is to his, but at least Funchal is one hell of a lot closer to UK than Toronto and that is very lucky for me."

They drove home and had a nightcap before going to bed and making love, but sometime around three in the morning, with Richard fast asleep beside her, Corinne was suddenly awake and full of doubt. 'What the hell am I doing here when all I really want is to be with Jonathan?' she asked herself. 'Now I've led Richard into believing he's just taken over where Jonathan left off, although he doesn't know it was only a couple of month ago. Be honest with yourself. You're not really over Jonathan yet. How can you be when you've only just split up?' she questioned herself. Suddenly thoughts of Jonathan overwhelmed her as Richard stirred in the bed beside her.

'Let's face it, I'm actually in an emotional mess and have been acting like a teenager on the rebound. That's my trouble, I simply bury my feelings so deep that when they do eventually surface, I can't handle them,' she chastised herself.

Yes, she had done a lot of grieving over Jonathon, so much so that her feelings for him had reduced to a dull ache.

Jetting off to be with Richard had certainly taken her mind off him, but now her feelings for him had suddenly resurfaced with a sort of longing for how it used to be. After all, they'd shared so much.

Corinne found it impossible to go back to sleep and when eventually, the darkened room grew faintly light, she slipped out of bed, gathered up her clothes and went into the old-fashioned bathroom to wash and dress before finding her way outside.

The sky was a pale blue and the sub-tropical garden was awash with bright colours of every hue, which only seemed to heighten her sense of melancholy. Making her way towards the ornate green Victorian seat overlooking Funchal and the ocean, she sat down and gazed into space as sounds of life drifted up from the town. "So there you are. I thought for a moment that you'd just upped and left me," he said coming around the seat and sitting down beside her. He was freshly showered and she could smell his aftershave. "Are you OK?" he asked, his voice now full of concern as it was obvious she was quite close to tears.

It was no good, she'd have to come out with it! "Look Richard, you really are a lovely, kind and generous man, but I think I've rather overstepped the mark by coming on to you so quickly. It's not your fault, it's all mine," she said, reaching out and taking his hand.

Suddenly, he was full of compassion, overwhelmed by the sadness in her eyes. "Look don't worry about it. I completely understand and I did think it was all moving a little too quickly, so let's just revert to being good friends for the rest of your stay," he suggested. "Oh, could we Richard?" she said, immediately beginning to feel her melancholy melting away.

"Of course we can, and now I'm definitely ready for our breakfast which Francis has already laid in the conservatory," he said.

After breakfast, they climbed aboard his powerful jeep, ideally suited to Madeira's mountainous landscape and he took her on an extensive tour of the island, winding up through the banana plantations and the fast growing eucalyptus forests and eventually ending up at Madeira's highest peak, Monte Pico Ruivo, which he told her, was at the third highest in Portugal.

When they eventually got back to the house, again, unseen hands had moved all her things back into the guest bedroom where Francis had even gone to the trouble of arranging her toothbrush and toothpaste in a holder on the side of the adjoining bathroom basin.

That evening they again dined in Funchal's old town, but kept their topics of conversation strictly neutral with Richard maintaining his demeanor of being just a very good friend, despite their earlier love making, so much so that Corinne began wondering if she'd overreacted to her emotions.

They spent the following couple of days walking Madeira's famous Levada water channel trails and dined at home in the evenings with Richard demonstrating his culinary abilities, a skill Jonathan had never mastered and had made no pretence about it.

The day before her scheduled noon departure, they took the cable car up to the spectacular Monte Palace and Madeira tropical gardens. Richard called Francis to come and pick them up in the jeep and take them to the less well known and much quieter Palheiro tropical gardens and parkland where they had lunch at a small open-air cafe in the grounds.

"You know I have really enjoyed our week together, more than you'll probably ever know," said Richard as he viewed the prospect of her jetting off in the morning leaving him to resume his single existence. Corinne saw this too and suddenly her heart went out to him. "Shall we go home and have a quiet evening listening to some music from your wonderful collection of vinyls and then perhaps spend our last night together?"

Somehow thoughts of Jonathan had lost their poignancy and going to bed with Richard, as a sort of farewell gesture now seemed to be the most natural thing in the world. "Yes, I'd like that very much," he replied.

They spoke little on the short drive back to the airport the following morning, each experiencing a feeling of unreality, as if the past week had all been something out of a bitter sweet dream. They hugged briefly in the busy departures hall, amid a moving sea of holiday makers pushing trolleys piled high with luggage, and then it was all over.

As the short haul Airbus charter holiday jet levelled off at its cruising altitude, Corinne looked down on the now tiny island floating in the vastness of the Atlantic Ocean and wondered if she'd made a mistake by ending their whirlwind romance.

Chapter 9

"Do you think we might start trying for a baby tonight?" Gloria suggested. She'd moved in with Jonathan several months earlier and it was now generally accepted at Joseph B Mayer and Sons, attorneys at law, that the latest and youngest partner to join their practice, the extremely bright, keen and attractive partner, Gloria Ann Delaney, had now scaled the heights and taken their boss's heart by storm. Some wondered what had happened to Jonathan's long-term relationship with the English woman he was always jetting off across the pond to visit, but none were close enough to him to ask and what did it matter anyway.

Gloria was wearing her sexiest underwear as she approached him, a bit like a slinky black cat stalking her prey. Jonathan, who was sitting up in bed reading, put down his book as she approached, the subject he'd been doing his level best to avoid for weeks now staring him uncomfortably in the face.

It was his own bloody fault because in the white heat of their romance, he'd led her to believe he wasn't against starting a family, after all he was forty-five and it was going to be now or never if his offspring were not going to have an old man as their dad, he'd rationalized. But since Gloria had moved in and had started radically changing his lifestyle, he'd come to realise that a domestic life and babies was something he needed like a hole in the head. That was not the only thing, because Gloria was also socially ambitious and had already begun manoeuvring them into social circles, which she thought appropriate for one of the leading legal firms in Toronto.

Jonathan, by nature, was more retiring and while attending all the official dinners and functions that were on the legal calendar, he made no attempt to go further than was necessary and had consequently gained the reputation of being a bit of a loner.

Now as the weeks living with Gloria had gone by, he'd come to realise that his former life, sharing confidences and regular lunches, dinners and fishing trips up to the camp with Shaun, and his evening Skypes and holidays with Corinne, was a life that perfectly suited him and like a fool, he'd thrown it all away.

He could not escape the fact that in the early days of his budding romance with Gloria, he had convinced himself that it was high time to settle down and start a family, but now he knew with an awful finality it was definitely not what he wanted and if he did not put an end to it right now it would be too late.

"Listen Gloria I have come to the conclusion that I actually don't want children." There he'd said it. "But that's not what you said earlier. In fact, you said that if we did not start soon, it would probably be too late. Those were your very words!" she reminded him. "Yes, I know they were and I truly meant it at the time," he conceded. "So, what's happened to change your mind?" she challenged. "Well, nothing really." It was a weak response and he knew it. "What do you mean by 'nothing really?' she challenged. "Look Gloria, I've come to realise over the past few months, that I'm not really the marrying and settling down type." A stony, ominous silence filled the space between them. "Well, you've left it a bit bloody late I must say." Now tears were welling up in her eyes. It was the one womanly weapon few men are able to resist and Jonathan was no exception. For a moment he hovered between giving way to her desires or standing firm. "I'm sorry because hurting you is the very last thing in the world I want to do," he said quietly, bowing his head as he did so. "Well, you've chosen a fine way of showing it I must say," she said turning around and flouncing out. "I'll sleep in the guest room tonight," she called back.

They breakfasted, got ready for work and drove to the office in a stony silence because there was no middle ground they could possibly share. It didn't take the other partners long to realise something was up and, as Shaun had predicted, after six of the most uncomfortable weeks Jonathan had ever experienced, Gloria had resigned and accepted another position with a law firm in Vancouver. He now had the big house to himself because his mother had gone to live with her sister. She had considered returning, but then decided she actually quite enjoyed living with her sister, who'd said she could stay as long as she liked.

Such is often the perversity of human nature, that once he was all by himself in the house, Jonathan found himself experiencing an emotion that up until then, he'd seldom felt, namely loneliness. Had giving up on Gloria, whom he'd hurt terribly deeply, been a dreadful mistake after all? He wandered into his den and poured himself a stiff whisky and sat there in his favourite brown leather chair quietly waiting for the effect of the alcohol to kick in. Did he have the nerve to call up Corinne and to confess that Gloria had been a terrible mistake? that was the question. It was then that his mobile burst into life. It was Shaun inviting himself around for a nightcap because he had a feeling his best buddy was in need of some company.

Five minutes later they were sitting opposite one

another, drinks in hand. "Well, she's finally gone then," observed Shaun raising his tumbler. "Yes, she's gone and I'm feeling a complete heal and you know the worst of it is that now its irrevocably over, I'm not sure I've done the right thing," he admitted. "That's a question to ask yourself a month from today and certainly not now when it's all so raw," said Shaun. They sat for a couple of moments in a companionable silence and then started reminiscing about the three weeks they'd spent with Corinne and Alicia that spectacular fall. "There's no doubt about it, those two woman had a profound effect on both of us?" said Shaun.

"Yes and I went and spoilt everything," retorted Jonathan now feeling even more morose. "Tell you what old buddy, when time allows, why don't we just throw caution to the wind, take a couple of weeks off, fly over to England and book ourselves into The Oreford under the Robert's brothers?" he suggested. "Take it from me, Corinne will be far more impressed if you fly three thousand miles to get down on bended knee and beg her forgiveness, rather than picking up the phone to her," he advised. "And as for me; Alicia may well be married, but I'm sure she she'd find a way to see me if she's too embarrassed to bring her husband along!" he added. "Shaun that's a plan, but where the hell did the Roberts brothers come from?" he asked. "Sorry old buddy. I haven't a clue."

Chapter 10

It was just over a month after Royston's death that Mark Hammond got in touch and left a message on her answerphone, as Alicia had predicted he surely would. And again, as she had foretold, he was suggesting he call around to discuss the estate agency business in which she'd retained a ten percent interest under the terms of her husband's will.

Alicia had spent her time gradually rediscovering what it was like to be single again after all these years, although either Annie or Bob had called around most days and both Heather and Hannah had made it their business to take her under their collective wing.

Anthony seemed to be getting over his father's tragic sudden death quite well, although he didn't say much. Bob had willingly accepted Alicia's suggestion that he take charge of the car collection and the two spent hours valeting the vintage and classic cars and going out for a spin, to take his mind off things.

Corina had eventually stopped asking for her daddy and her little life had more or less returned to normal.

Now Alicia was being put on the spot by Mark, who certainly had a polite, but persuasive way when talking on the telephone.

It was all right for Corinne to say that if she didn't want to see him, then to keep putting him off until he got the message, but that was certainly easier said than done. And was she so sure she definitely did not want to think of him as a future partner? Surely the jury was out for the moment and the best course was still to adopt a wait and see policy.

She'd been really upset for Corinne when Jonathan had dumped her. After Royston's death it had crossed her mind that the two of them would be foot lose and fancy free together, but now she was in Madeira with her new man, so that had certainly changed the dynamics.

Once or twice over the past month it had also crossed her mind to get in touch with Shaun, who was, she'd instinctively known all along, Corina's real father. She'd grown ever more certain of this as the child slowly emerged from babyhood. There were no indications in her physical appearance, which thank God, had never given Royston any reason to suspect that the child was other than his own, but as she began developing into a little person, certain mannerisms started emerging that were unmistakably Shaun's.

Their full-on holiday romance had been such an intense experience it had seared itself into her whole being at some deeper level and was why she was so easily seeing her former lover in her child. But contacting Shaun and telling him he had a daughter, could only result in a whole lot of complications and would inevitably lead to her being painted as the unfaithful wife of a kind, loving and generous man, whom many people had held in such high regard. Just what would Bob, Annie, Hannah and Heather, who had gone out of their way to support her over these past few weeks, think of her for a start?

No, contacting Shaun in the hope he would make everything feel better, did not even bear thinking about. Alicia knew that if she ignored Mark's message, he'd think that she hadn't received it and call again so that was completely pointless.

So, she would call him, but do her level best to keep everything strictly on a business footing by arranging to meet him in the Draymarket estate agency office and not here at home.

Chapter 11

When Mark picked up Alicia's message via an email from one of
the sales negotiators in Royston Randall and Company's Draymarket office, suggesting he meet her there and giving him a couple of optional dates, he was not best pleased to say the least, It had immediately shattered his cosy image of them sitting together on opposite sides of her breakfast bar, or better still in her comfortable lounge, while talking business. possibly over a cuppa, or even better a glass of wine. He'd even planned to bring along an expensive classic car model as a gift for Anthony, with whom he knew he got on rather well. But now all those plans had come to naught and he didn't like it because he was used to people being compliant and doing his bidding and not
thwarting his arrangements. Still, if that was how she wanted to play it, then he'd let her know again, via that sales negotiator, that those dates were not convenient and that they'd have to postpone their meeting until another time because there was no
way he was going to be at her beck and call because that was definitely not the natural order of things in his world.

Mark continued scanning through the thirty or so other messages that had flooded in during his late afternoon boardroom meeting with four new Austrian and German investors keen to join his consortium. They had been impressed following his spectacular success taking a controlling interest in a prospecting company that had just confirmed a substantial new gold deposit in Nicaragua, whereupon their share capital had gone through the ceiling.

While his substantial financial links with the, shady Jimarenal Corporation had been severed when they'd hurriedly withdrawn their investment, he had, through another remarkable stroke of good fortune, recently made a highly profitable connection with a former corporation insider, who had left the business and was at this moment jetting in from San Jose, Costa Rica.

She was one Gabriella Lopez, the former, then much younger mistress of the now deceased Edelmira Sanchez, who had tipped Mark off on the gold investment opportunity and now wanted to meet him in person to discuss what else she could bring to the table. She also wanted to be there when he made the agreed transfer of two million dollars US into her newly opened Swiss bank account as her commission payment for services rendered. She would be accompanied by her PA, one Angelina Perez, alias Chrissy Morales, who had risen through the ranks to become a senior member of the Costa Rican serious crime squad.

It was Chrissy, working with Carlos Diaz, a new and dynamic boss, who'd eventually tracked down Gabriella and had made her an offer she could not refuse, namely to tell all she knew about the corporation's narcotics production and money laundering operations right across the region in exchange for immunity from prosecution. Gabriella had not taken too much persuading, seeing that Brad Meyer, her close confidant for many years, had done nothing to stop her being eased out by his twenty-three-year-old son as soon as he'd joined his father at the head of the corporation. There had been no love lost between the two because Brad Junior blamed her for being responsible for his parents' parting and eventual divorce. It was her information that had led to the arrest of Brad Meyer Junior at his father's funeral and that of a whole bag of corrupt politicians and senior officials, who had been on the receiving end of more than generous donations from the corporation in respect of services rendered.

But Chrissy's new boss was out to make an international name for himself and what better way than to bring down the head of one of the world's most successful hedge funds.

His team had very quickly discovered that the Jimarenal Corporation had made a huge investment in Mark Hammond's fund some years earlier and had later withdrawn it. But there was no hard evidence to suggest Mark had knowingly accepted their tainted investment. What was required now was a honey trap to secure the evidence, if there was any, and who better to bait it then one Chrissy Morales, who'd always believed that in the pursuit of justice any means justified the end. But there was no need to rush, so maybe just gain his trust and establish her credentials as Gabriella's PA on this visit and then spring the confirmatory trap on some future occasion.

Gabriella had retired to an exclusive beach resort on the Caribbean coast of Columbia. Now in her mid-seventies, she had retained her striking good looks and, like many a wealthy film star, had the resources to stem the natural ageing process, so much so, that she also possessed what she called the gasp factor if anyone discovered her age.

Gabriella had assumed that once her vital insider information had brought down the Jimarenal Corporation, that would have been the end of the matter, but no, Carlos Diaz had come back for more. Now she had been coerced into making contact with a wealthy UK hedge fund boss and to offer him a deal too tempting to turn down, and that was going to require a flight to Zurich.

Mark occupied a staffed penthouse suit with its own boardroom in a luxury managed apartment block in the centre of Zurich when he was 'in town,' which was at least once a month. It was here he entertained potential investors, business associates and guests, but it was not to be the venue for his meeting with Gabriella and her assistant. They were booked in to the adjoining luxury hotel and he had arranged to meet them in the cocktail bar around 7pm before going on to dine in its Michelin star restaurant.

Mark had always been instinctively cautious when it came to new people offering him their services and suggesting investment opportunities that might look to be too good to be true.

He had taken up the investment advice from Gabriella because of her close links with the corporation and that had certainly reaped a rich reward, but now he wished to know more about her before admitting her to his inner circle and far better to do that on neutral territory.

Mark, smart brown leather laptop case in hand, wandered casually into the bar just after the appointed time and immediately spotted the two raven-haired women sitting discreetly in a small alcove.

The older woman, he judged to be in her mid-sixties and still extremely attractive, but there was something disconcerting about the way her eyes were drilling into him the

moment they met. Her associate was probably around thirty and could only be described as strikingly handsome, but had a more open and friendly face. They both rose to greet him as he approached and shook hands, whereupon Mark suggested they move to the far more intimate surroundings of a neighbouring suite of comfortable armchairs. They had yet to order drinks, so Mark summoned a nearby waiter, with whom he was on friendly first name terms, and once their order was taken, they settled into the customary first meeting small talk regime.

So how was their flight and were the two adjoining rooms he had booked for them, OK? he enquired. It wasn't long before they got down to business and Gabriella began expanding on potential areas of future investment. Chrissy sat attentively by her side saying very little, but giving Mark knowing looks, which he found both enticing and a little distracting.

There were breaks in the conversation while Mark's waiter served their drinks and then when the restaurant maitre d came out with the menus and later to take their orders. It was just after he'd withdrawn that Mark casually picked up and opened his laptop and made the cash transfer to Gabriella.

Chrissy watched on impassively, knowing that was more money earned from a simple exchange of information than she would earn in years. Once the transaction had been completed and Gabriella had come to the end of her informal presentation, they moved into the subtly lit high end restaurant and everyone began to relax.

Gabriella related the agreed cover story that she'd met her collegue at a business conference in Panama City and really hit it off, so much so that Angelina had decided to resign her position as PA to one of the conference key-note speakers and join Gabriella.

She and Mark went on to discuss the general state of affairs in the world financial markets and on the political situations in the major player nations that inevitably impacted on the price of key commodities in one way or another. He was impressed by her depth of knowledge when it came to Central and South America and the

Caribbean and decided that as far as future investments in that part of the world were concerned, she was worth her weight in gold. As they rose to leave, and acting on an impulse perhaps fuelled by drinking a little more than he'd intended, he invited them across the road to his business suite for a

nightcap. Somewhat to his surprise, Gabriella made the excuse that she was now feeling the effects of a long flight and would retire, but that Angelina might wish to join him. Knowing this was the opportunity she'd been waiting for, Chrissy politely accepted

the invitation. On the way back to his suite, Mark explained that Zurich had become the European hub of his operations over recent years, and therefore he found it both convenient and cost effective to maintain a staffed presence. The resident staff, namely one Jacob Johnson, had retired to his adjoining apartment for the night and his PA Adel, who would normally be using one of the four guest bedrooms, was conveniently out in the country staying with friends for a couple of days, so they had the place to themselves.

Mark went to his well-stocked drinks cabinet and asked Chrissy what she would have. She replied that she was happy with whatever he was having. "In that case it will have to be a small brandy with ice as I am very conscious of the fact that I have already consumed more than my business entertainment quota and I will have to see you back to the hotel shortly," he replied. "So, let me give you the in-house tour," he added, leading her through the luxurious lounge area with its range of leather sofas and armchairs and into his boardroom, the centrepiece of which was a long highly polished natural pine table. At the far end was a huge screen which he moved casually towards, picked up a remote and activated. It came to life, displaying a series of sections giving the state of play of all the major markets currently open and operating around the world.

Chrissy immediately saw the significance of it, even with were untrained eyes, and for some reason it both intrigued and excited her. Maybe it was because she had earlier witnessed Gabriella receiving all that money for just one exchange of information.

Suddenly her resolve to bring this man down by deceiving him, weakened. After all, they actually had nothing, other than circumstantial evidence, against him. She was there to trick him into revealing something incriminating so that her boss
could make a name for himself, while her reward would be nothing more than a pat on the back and being told what a clever girl she was. No, she wasn't going down

that road because she was finding herself attracted to this obviously fabulously wealthy man with his penthouse business suit and private jet.

He was softly spoken, polite and self-deprecating and it would certainly be exciting to be part of his life.

"That's pretty impressive, so what are all these prices telling you?" she asked. Put on the spot, he began explaining country by country, what the figures displayed on the screen were telling him. "So, tell me, how much cash you could make from what you are seeing right now?" she asked. "That's the market traders' game, but seeing that's where I cut my teeth in this business, let's see what we can do," he replied.

Over the next thirty minutes, Mark bought and sold stock while keeping up a running commentary and then closed down having increased his personal fortune by around 20,000 US dollars.

"That's amazing Mark," said Chrissy with genuine admiration.

"But I guess it's time I was going." It was not what she said, but the way that she said it that left Mark in no doubt that she didn't have to go, if he would prefer her to stay. He hesitated. "Yes, it is pretty late to get you back to the hotel, so you are most welcome to use one of our guest bedrooms tonight and we could go back to the hotel for breakfast in the morning," he suggested.

"If you're sure that won't be an inconvenience, then that would be great because, to tell you the truth, it's been a long day and I am feeling pretty tired," she confessed.

Mark led the way to the room and turned and bid her goodnight, making no attempt to enter in the pretence of showing her where everything was, the obvious move had he been thinking of seducing her.

In truth, he had, but changed his mind at the last moment because, like his play for the lovely Alicia, this seduction could also be handled at his leisure, he contemplated as he walked slowly back to his own suite. But with Alicia suddenly back in his thoughts, Mark changed his mind about continuing to ignore her and resolved to instruct William Weaver to send around a large bouquet of flowers, together with a note of apology for not getting in touch
personally, and also to source a suitable classic car model for Anthony.

Chapter 12

"Hello dear Little Oreford. It's been a long day, but I'm pleased to be home," Corinne said out loud as she finally emerged from the leafy lane and into the village.

It was a perfect early summer evening and all was as she'd left it, what seemed like ages ago, but was only just over a week.

As she drove slowly past the Inn, the first thing to catch her eye was her magnificent hanging basket displays of bright red geraniums and in an instant, she was thinking of dear Richard and his beautiful tropical garden.

Annie on reception, gave her a warm welcome, telling her that all had run smoothly during her absence and that Laura had called, wanting her to pop around for a chat as soon as she got back. Entering her apartment and putting down her case, she saw at once that her answerphone was blinking. Her impulse was to ignore it until she'd had a long hot soak in the bath, but then thought better of it. The first message was from Laura asking her to pop over because she had some important family news, and the second was from Richard, hoping she'd got home safely. There was a further call from Michael Silver, suggesting another evening at The Cheringford Arms, and finally, a message from Alicia, hoping she'd had a great time and wondering when she might be free to pop over for a catch up as she couldn't wait to hear how it had all gone with Richard. All these demands when all she really wanted was a long soak, followed by a light supper sent over from the kitchen and an early night.

Corinne was just about to enter the bath when the wall phone rang and she hovered between answering or ignoring it.

A second later, she'd answered it and then wished she hadn't because it was Laura again, asking her to come over because there was some important family news she needed to share with her and that it was not all good. "Look Sis, can't this really wait until tomorrow because I've been travelling all day and all I really want is a bath and to climb into bed." There was a moment's silence. "I'm not sure it should, especially as it partly concerns The Oreford," her sister replied. "OK I'll be over in an hour," Corinne promised, replacing the receiver in its cradle and climbing into the bath. I'm going to enjoy this soak and while I'm having it, I'm not going to think about Richard or Michael or Jonathan, or anything,' she resolved.

"So, what's this news that's so important it just couldn't have waited until tomorrow?" Corinne asked Laura and

Ben once she'd told them briefly about her holiday. "All right, we'll come straight to the point and then you'll see why we needed to break this news now rather than waiting until tomorrow," said Laura, looking at Ben for support. "Lottie and Andy were around for supper last night and told us that they were thinking seriously about upping sticks and leaving Little Oreford," they explained.
"Why on earth should they want to do that?" Corinne asked, instantly realising the implications for the family and for The Oreford of losing its, now almost indispensable, son-in-law head chef.
"Mum's going to be really upset if they take the twins away from her now, surely they can see that?" she pointed out. "I would have thought they have work and family life about as good as it can possibly get," she added. Ben said that was certainly true from his and Laura's perspective.
"But I can also see it from their point of view, because while they really do appreciate that they have pretty much the perfect lifestyle at the moment, Andy feels he has more to prove in pursuing his career. If they carry on as they are, things will be more or less the same ten years from now and I have to agree that he's probably right about that," he admitted.
Now her recent evening with the attentive and former

highly experienced head chef, Michael Silver, popped into Corinne's head and almost instantly, she'd thought of a plan.

Her soak in the bath had calmed her down, but now she was fuelled with an adrenalin rush that can sometimes occur when one passes through the sleep barrier.

"I can think of a way we can help Andy meet his career aspirations without the family having to pull up sticks and move away from Little Oreford," she told them. "You can," said Laura, looking across at Ben. "Yes, instead of being in charge, Andy is obviously yearning to spend time working under some inspirational Michelin Star head chef in the white heat of some top hotel kitchen or famous restaurant where he can hone his skills and develop his obvious talent," she pointed out. "From what Andy was saying to us last night, I think you've hit the nail smack on the head Corinne, but how can we make that happen without them having to move away from Little Oreford?" asked Ben.

"What we do is to hire a good temporary chef for The Oreford and allow Andy to take a year's paid sabbatical, working for free if necessary, under some top chefs around the country," she suggested, "It's the perfect solution. How clever of you to think of it," said Ben.

"It's not that clever because I happened to have supper a couple of weeks ago with Michael Silver, a former chef, who'd worked in top hotels and on cruise liners before taking over as catering department principle at the North Devon College. He's going to be sending some work experience students to us, so I guess all this just got stirred around in my head. On top of that, I'm sure Michael would have some valuable contacts in the hotel and catering industry if Andy and Lottie go for our compromise.

So, if you're in agreement, I'll have a chat with Andy after the luncheon service tomorrow," she suggested. "Corinne that's brilliant, so of course we're in agreement aren't we Ben?" It then occurred to Corinne to mention the possibility of acquiring The Cheringford Arms, where she'd met up with Michael, but then decided to leave that until a less complicated time and instead asked if any plans had been made for Charlie's forthcoming birthday. "Yes, we have, but first we have to tell you our other important news," said Laura. "!'m not sure I can take any more news right now, but go on then," said Corinne. "The day after you flew out to Madeira, Luke and his new partner Roxanne joined us for supper and, right out of the blue, they told us they wanted to get married and that, what's more they wanted it to be as soon as possible in our church with a marquee reception on the lawn here at Albany House," she explained. "That certainly is important news," said Corinne, instantly wondering if Roxanne was pregnant hence the indecent haste. "So what do you both think of that?" she asked, knowing her sister wasn't overly keen on her son's latest, quite outspoken, partner.

Laura had much preferred his former long-term girlfriend, who'd eventually left him because he was still reluctant to get married and settle down. "They're both climatologists and passionate about the need to fight climate change and they seem very happy together, so as she's Luke's choice, we have to do everything we can to support them, don't we Laura?" said Ben, pointedly.

Once back in her apartment, Corinne sent texts to Richard and Michael and went to bed. She spent the following morning catching up on paperwork and had a long chat with Andy after the lunchtime service. "I'd hate the family to think for a single moment that I'm in any way ungrateful for the wonderful working and home life that has opened up for me since I came here from college and met Lottie," said Andy, after he'd taken of his whites and they were sitting together over a coffee in a quiet corner of the bar. "But unless something happens, we could be sitting here having this same conversation ten years from now and professionally I will have advanced no further, and I am beginning to feel uncomfortable about that," he admitted.

"Lottie and I have spent hours talking about the situation. She would, of course, be terribly reluctant to give up all that we have here in order for me to take up a new post with prospects. But she's willing to give it a try, because as she says, if it didn't work out, we do have the luxury of coming home," he pointed out.

"Well, there is an alternative Andy, which I hope you don't mind, I discussed with Laura and Ben last night after they told me of your plans. There is nothing I would like more than to see The Oreford awarded a Michelin Star.

But realistically, that's never going to be possible, until you go out into the world and gain the skills and inspiration you need, working under the top chefs in your industry to make it happen."

She could see she had now captured his full attention.

"So, what we are proposing is that you take a year's fully paid sabbatical to give you that opportunity, which means that Lottie and the twins do not need to be uprooted from their home and school. Lottie would then be free to join you at weekends and on your days off because, goodness knows you have a whole family of child minders at your disposal," she smiled, as she watched him consider all that she had suggested. "Do you think this could really work?" he asked. She could tell by the tone of his voice that he would jump at the opportunity. "I can't see why ever not, especially as you would be offering your years of proven experience free of charge. You would, of course, have to interview and choose your successor here, which I am sure would not be a problem. "But where would the money be coming from to fund my sabbatical and pay my stand-in?" he asked.

"It would come from the Jameson Family Trust Fund, which as you know, was set up by Charlie and Lottie's adopted Uncle and Aunt, Robin and Margo, to allow Laura, Ben and I to use a proportion of our future inheritance to expand and develop the business," she explained. "If you and Laura and Ben are sure about this, then it's an amazing offer and I simply don't know how to thank you," he replied, "Don't worry about thanking us now, just go home and ask Lottie what she thinks," said Corinne, glancing at her watch and realising she was now running late for her afternoon catch-up with Alicia.

But then she was waylaid by Annie, who needed to discuss a double booking, so it was another twenty minutes before she was able to get away.

"To tell you the truth Alicia, I feel in a complete emotional mess and I don't like it," Corinne confessed. They were sitting together over two large glasses of freshly squeeze orange juice, while her goddaughter Corina played happily with her dolls' house on the kitchen floor. Anthony was up in his room deeply engrossed in a game he was playing remotely with Michael. "I suppose the truth is, I was completely mad to go off to Madeira and raise all poor Richard's hopes before I'd had enough time to get over Jonathan, and now Michael's come on the scene and clearly wants to be more that a friend, unless I'm completely wrong in reading the signs. But that's quite enough about me, so how are you feeling Alicia?" she asked. "Touche, because I'm also in an emotional muddle, really missing Royston, one minute and then beginning to think it's quite nice being my own person again, the next. And now, right out of the blue, I've had this letter from Peter, the guy I had a previous long term on and off relationship with," she revealed. "I don't think you've ever told me about him," said Corinne, feeling mildly surprised. "No, I haven't and that's because I was still seeing him occasionally when I moved to Hampton Green to teach at the village school and Royston came along. Peter was the reason why Royston went on seeing that maniac Tanya Talbot, who did those terrible things to us when she found us together in his bungalow," she explained.

"I can understand your wanting to put him and that whole terrible incident behind you, so what does Peter say in the letter and how on earth did he know your address after all this time?"

"He didn't. He just happened to see a small piece about Royston's death in the papers and rang the Gazette and spoke to Jackie Benson, who said if he wrote to her, she'd pass the letter on, so that's what happened," she explained, "So, what does he say?" she asked. "Not a lot, other than he was sorry to hear of Royston's death and that, believe it or not, he was still single and often thought about me and that if I'd like to meet up with him at some point for old time's sake, then to give him a call," she explained.

"Look at Corina playing all by herself over there, completely happy in her own world, so do you think she has the secret and that we need to be completely OK in ourselves without men," Alicia asked. "I think that's a lot easier said than done," replied Corinne, suggesting they should take her goddaughter on a stroll up to the lookout. "I don't suppose Anthony's going to want to come, is he?" she asked. "No, Bob's due over shortly because they're doing some maintenance work on one of the cars."

They returned in the late afternoon, just as the local florist drove up to deliver a large bouquet from Mark Hammond, together with his apology note. It was while they were having afternoon tea on the patio with Bob and Anthony, that a second van delivered a parcel addressed to Master Anthony Randall and containing a top of the range replica Daimler model. It was clear to Alicia that her son was highly delighted, but one glance at Bob told her that he was thinking exactly what she was thinking.

Corinne and Alicia returned to the topic of 'men' after Corina was in bed and Anthony, having devoured a whole suppertime pizza, was now back in his room again playing yet another game on his ipad with Michael.
"Corina's actually Shaun's child, I'm convinced of that now," Alicia said after they'd been talking for a couple of minutes about how her small daughter was now definitely her own little person.

"Are you really sure?" Corinne asked. "Well of course, I wasn't at first because she's never actually looked like him, thank God, but as she's grown, I've started spotting all sorts of different little mannerisms, which are definitely Shaun's, and were never Royston's. While you've been away, I've been getting myself more and more into a muddle over whether or not I should call him and tell him he's got a daughter, because once I had, there would be no way back and who knows how he might react and what complications it would create." She paused. "Then there's the question of what all our close friends would think of me cheating on darling Royston the first minute I got the chance three thousand miles away from here?" she pointed out.

"I think you'd have to be absolutely sure before you went down that road. As you so rightly say, it could lead to all sorts of complications with Shaun possibly wanting access to Corina and what if you then discovered you were not that keen on him after all? But I'm sure Annie and Bob and Hannah and Heather would certainly not hold it against you, if you told them in advance and were completely open and honest with them," Corinne assured her. "So does this mean that Mark Hammond is definitely out of the frame now?" she asked. "Well, that's where I have been getting myself into another muddle. He called to invite himself around and left a message on the answerphone and I rang the Draymarket office and suggested a couple of dates when we could meet up there and not here.

I got a terse reply back, via one of his team, saying that the dates were not suitable and that he'd be back in touch. Now that huge bouquet has arrived with that expensive classic car model for Anthony." Alicia got up and went back into the kitchen to refill their glasses with white wine, before returning to the question of Mark Hammond. "I don't want to be rude to him, especially as he was Royston's friend and his agreement to acquire the business would have set him free to enjoy his retirement. So, I think I'm going to do my best to keep him as a friend and to maybe make it clear to him that that is all I want," she resolved. "I'll drink to that," said Corrine, raising her glass.

Chapter 13

When Chrissy emerged from her suite around 7.30am, having made herself as presentable as possible, and walked through into the spacious lounge, it was empty, but there were domestic sounds coming from the adjoining kitchen. Not knowing quite what to do next, she walked over the panoramic window and gazed out across the city.

"Ah there you are Miss Perez, Good morning." Chrissy turned to face a man, she'd guess in his early fifties, and wearing a stylish black jacket and matching trousers. "I'm Jacob and I manage the apartment for Mr Hammond and organise his business diary while he's here in Zurich. Unfortunately, some unexpected business has come up and he's busy in the boardroom, so he has asked me to escort you back to the hotel where he hopes to join you later." Jacob chatted easily on their short drive back to the hotel and happily answered her questions about the Zurich. She'd already showered, so it only took a few minutes to redo her makeup, change and go down to the restaurant where she quickly spotted Gabriella sitting by herself at a table for two in the window looking out over the city and went over to join her.

"So how was your evening and did you achieve all that you had intended?" she asked almost as soon as Chrissy had sat down and picked up the elaborate breakfast menu. There was a coldness in her voice, as if she despised the deceit forced upon her by Chrissy and her boss back in San Jose.

Gabriella now had her cash safely in her new Swiss bank account, so could fly back to Costa Rica and then on to Columbia and forget all about Mark Hammond. She'd fulfilled her side of the bargain by contacting this hedge fund boss and offering him an irresistible investment opportunity, sourced by a couple of calls to former contacts, and had allowed this woman to accompany her. They had a flight home booked for late afternoon and, as far as she was concerned, that was going to be the end of their association, the only redeeming factor being the large commission she had earned.

Gabriella's unfriendly tone was not lost on Chrissy. They'd spoken little on the flight over with her being left in no doubt that the former Jimarenal Corporation insider resented her presence. However, now she'd made up her mind not to attempt an entrapment of Mark, might there be some common ground between them, she wondered? But before she had any more time to contemplate the question, he'd arrived and was standing over them, apologising for being late and suggesting they move to a larger table before they ordered. Gabriella explained that she'd already had her breakfast and would now be going up to prepare for her departure. "It's been a real pleasure meeting you Mark and I very much look forward to working with you in the future," she lied, standing up and extended him her hand. "Angelina would you be happy to make your own way to the airport this afternoon?" Chrissy hesitated. "Actually, Gabriella, Zurich looks to be and amazing city and as this is my first visit to Europe, I think I might stay on for a few more days," she heard herself saying.

"That's certainly fine by me," she replied, giving Mark a courteous nod before turning her back on them and walking away. "So now we have the day to ourselves and I'd be delighted to take a little time off to show you around," said Mark, suddenly pleased at the way things were turning out.

He'd regretted not coming on to this highly attractive young woman, who was clearly up for it, the previous evening and now, right out of the blue, he was being given a second opportunity.   Over breakfast, Chrissy told him all about her life growing up in Costa Rica and how after studying art and design at university and finding it impossible to get a job, she'd taken a secretarial course and drifted into the world of commerce. The first part of her story was all true. Yes, she had taken that secretarial course, but her first job had been with the police and from there she had never looked back, until now! They'd arranged to meet back at reception in an hour to begin their sightseeing tour and Chrissy was in a state of high excitement at the prospect of spending the day in the company of this fabulously wealthy man, whom she instinctively knew fancied her, hopefully as much as she did him. She changed out of her business suit and into the only casual wear she'd brought for the trip, comprising a dark red top, which emphasised her copper skin and sleek long ebony coloured hair, and a matching flowing skirt, which finished provocatively, just above the knee. Not bringing a bigger wardrobe had been a mistake. which would have to be rectified by going shopping at her first opportunity if she was going to spend more time with Mark Hamond. He was already waiting in reception when she emerged from an empty lift and walked out into the foyer and across to him, looking absolutely stunning.

Heads turned and this was not lost on Mark, who rose and spontaneously kissed her on the cheek, a signal to those all around that she was his. They spent the whole day and evening together, both knowing that ending up in bed was now inevitable. "Do you have to go back to Costa Rica?" he asked the following morning after one final love making session, as leaning up on one elbow, he gazed into her brown eyes. "Not if you don't want me too Mark, but I'd need to find a job," she replied. "That's easily solved because you could come and work with me," he answered. "I'd happily help you with your administration, but I'd want to learn all about your share dealing and other operations and really become part of your world, because I found all that you showed me on your screen last night, absolutely fascinating," she said and he knew she meant it.

Later that morning, he introduced her to his UK PA Adel and announced that she would now be assisting Jacob with administrative and other duties here in Zurich. The two women politely shook hands. Adel gave Chrissy a genuine welcoming smile, knowing perfectly well what other duties she'd be performing for her insatiable boss. Jacob, who returned from an errand a few minutes later, was delighted at the unexpected prospect of having such a highly attractive assistant for company, especially as he had warmed to her on their short car ride back to the hotel the previous morning. "Will you be occupying one of the guest suits?" he asked, looking at his boss for confirmation. For some reason the question as to where she would live had yet to surface in the whirlwind maelstrom of the last twenty-four hours.

But Chrissy suddenly knew that living in that luxury penthouse would be claustrophobic and the very last thing that she wanted.

"Oh no, I will be staying on at the hotel until I can find a small apartment of my own," she replied firmly.

It was late afternoon when Mark Hammond and Adel took off in his private jet bound for London City Airport. Settling back in his plush leather armchair with a glass of fine red wine, as was his custom, while his personal chef prepared one of his favourite dishes, Mark considered that everything had tuned out rather well. He had a highly attractive and extremely eager assistant established in Zurich and now his thoughts were free to return to the delicious prospect of seducing the rather lovely widow, Alicia Randall.

Chapter 14

Making love with Roxanne in Luke's bedroom in Albany House always had to be a restrained affair because although his parents' room was as on the other side of the spacious landing, the noise of bouncing bed springs and the reciprocation of creaking floorboards created a sound that strangely carried through the old Victorian rectory. Normally it did not matter because he had moved into Roxanne's converted loft apartment in central London some months earlier, but being under his parents' roof called for some measure of restraint, even though he knew they were generally broad-minded about such things. The London apartment had been acquired for Roxanne by her widowed father, a Harley Street consultant surgeon, as an investment opportunity and because it meant that when his wayward daughter was in the country and not off around the world on some climate change mission, then at least there were opportunities for seeing a little more of one another.
It was now just after midnight and, passion sated, they were cuddled up together in Luke's double bed and talking in whispers about the day ahead when Roxanne's father would be driving down to stay at The Oreford Inn and to meet Luke's parents for the first time.

Luke said it was all going to be fine, but Roxanne was not quite so reassured because she'd picked up the vibe that her prospective mother-in-law had not really taken to her.

Then there was the question of their forthcoming wedding, which was part of the reason for his visit. Had it been left to the two of them, it would have been a quiet register office affair with close family and a few of their friends and colleagues.

But that was not what her father wanted after they'd had broken the news to him over dinner at his favourite Michelin Star French restaurant in Central London, where owing to his many visits, he was a particularly favoured guest.

Dr Albert Flavell had been introduced to Luke some months earlier and, unlike Laura's reservations about her prospective daughter-in-law, he had taken to Luke almost immediately, seeing that both he and his daughter were clearly kindred spirits, full of enthusiasm for life and their beloved cause. Their obvious closeness so reminded him of the inseparable bond that both he and his beloved wife Edwina had forged in the months following their meeting at medical school, a life time ago. If Dr Albert Flavell was sure of anything, then it was that his precious daughter had found her soulmate and her partner for life in Luke Jameson, whom he could see, had a sensible head on his shoulders and just the right temperament to counter that of his daughter's quite volatile nature. But if they were going to be married then no, it was not going to be a quiet affair and on that he was not going to be moved. "This is a time of celebration for your parents Luke and, of course for me, and I do hope that you won't deny me the opportunity of making my father of the bride's speech in appropriate surroundings will you Roxanne?"

Despite all her wayward nature and her travelling around the world, her father had always been her rock, until Luke had come along, and if he wanted them to have a big wedding, then that's exactly what they would have, even though it would be a bit of a wasteful expense as far as saving the planet was concerned.

Unknown to him, he already had one supporter, whom he had yet to meet, that being Luke's indefatigable grandmother and confidant Charlie, who'd immediately warmed to Roxanne as a kindred wayward spirit almost as soon as they'd first met.

Dr Flavell, Laura and Ben Jameson, quickly discovered, was a genial, easy-going man of the world with an authoritative air, which was the perfect combination of qualities needed when it came to building up a considerable client base for his Harley Street consultancy, where he was a leading authority in his field.

Luke had suggested to his mother that they should meet his prospective father-in-law over lunch in The Oreford restaurant. This, he pointed out, would spare all the stress of having to prepare and serve a meal and they could then all go back to Albany House and relax over afternoon tea on the patio as the weather was still set fair.

The luncheon was a complete success with Roxanne's father holding court and regaling them with stories from his professional life. Corinne joined them all for coffee and walked back with them to Albany House, where Lottie and Andy had already arrived with Charlie, but without their boisterous twins, who'd conveniently been taken off for a play day with friends.

"What a lovely home you have," Dr Flavell had exclaimed as he was being given the grand tour by Laura and Ben. He got on extremely well with Charlie, as was expected, because of her generally welcoming and extrovert nature, and it was early evening by the time he finally made his excuses and left saying he had a little work on his laptop that was now requiring his attention.

Roxanne walked back with him to the inn, it having been agreed that she and Luke would take him off on a tour of the North Devon coast the following morning.

"I think that that all went off rather well, don't you?" said Ben as he and Laura, finally climbed into bed with two mugs of Earl Grey tea, which they always placed on their respective period bedside cabinets alongside the current books they were reading.

The wedding day had been fixed for three months hence, being the second Saturday in October, and their son's perspective father-in-law had insisted that he would be picking up the tab for everything, if he could leave it to them, with Luke and Roxanne's help, to make all the arrangements.

"The first thing we're going to have to do Ben is to book the marquee," said Laura, who was already getting into operation wedding mode, all reservations about her perspective daughter-in-law, now blown away.

Charlie, Lottie and Andy had all been impressed by Dr Albert Flavell and discussed all the happenings of that memorable afternoon as they drove slowly back through the lanes to Little Oreford Court. "I'm not quite sure how the conversation got around to it," said Andy. "But I was telling him all about our future plans and he told me he was a patron of the French Michelin Star restaurant

Emile's in central London. He's on first name terms with the multi-award-winning French chef and he's sure, he could obtain me an honorary position if that was what I wanted," he told them. "And what's more, if that did work out, then I could stay with him in his Harley Street apartment when I was working in town as he had plenty of room," he added.

"Andy that's simply amazing, so you must tell him you're really interested," said Lottie excitedly. "I already have. I know I should have waited and talked it over with you first, but it just seemed best to strike while the iron was hot," he explained. "I'm really glad you did and I've got a bit of news for you too in that Roxanne wants to have our twins as her page boys," she revealed.

Chapter 15

When Corinne got back to her apartment, there were two messages on her answerphone. The first was from Richard in Madeira suggesting they should Skype, say at 10pm the following evening, and the second was from Michael inviting her to meet up for another meal at The Cheringford Arms the following Sunday lunchtime.
She was not sure where, continuing to stay in touch with Richard was going to lead, as he was clearly lonely and in search of a wife, which she knew now that she could never be, although he was such a lovely man. She could not face the prospect of finally breaking it off with him over Skype, so she simply texted him saying she was terribly busy at the moment, but would catch up with him in a couple of weeks, although she knew she would probably not be keeping her promise. Then on an impulse, and although it was getting on for 10pm, she returned Michael's call and by the sound of his voice, he was delighted to hear from her. They chatted on for nearly an hour with Corinne telling him all about her day and Luke and Roxanne's wedding plans and he telling her about all the on-going preparatory work he still had to do for next term, even though the college was now closed until early September.

"People think those working in education always have long holidays, but mostly that's a complete myth," he said.

"Anyway, talking of leisure time, there are some lovely wooded walks to be done around Cheringford, so if you have a pair of walking boots, then I thought we could do one of them next Sunday afternoon," he suggested.

Corinne said that was a lovely idea and she was looking forward to it already. Things were developing quite nicely with Michael, she thought, as she finally climbed into bed.

It had rained heavily overnight on the following Sunday and the lovely wooded walks Michael had enthused about were now all slippery. They'd changed into their boots at the back of their cars in a small deserted car park after lunch and were now making their way carefully up a nearby hidden path to reach, what Michael had described as a tremendous view point, although Corinne doubted it would be as magnificent as the one from the top of Royston's lookout. 'Poor old Royston," she thought.

"I'm amazed at just how slippery this path is, considering we've had weeks and weeks of dry weather," said Michael, leading the way up the hill and telling her to be careful as the next section was particularly steep and difficult underfoot. Turning towards her as he was speaking, he lost his balance and began sliding back down the path towards her. Corinne instinctively opened her arms to stop him, but the weight of his body was too much and the next moment they were both on the ground with Michael on top of her. Somehow, they'd fallen sideways into a think clump of myrtle bushes bordering the path, which had easily broken their fall and after a couple of seconds regained their senses.

"We'll simply have to stop meeting like this," said Michael, his face just a few inches above hers. She lifted her head and in the next instant they were kissing passionately. Michael knew the small path he'd chosen was little used so there wasn't much chance that anyone would come upon them.

They were both only wearing light waterproof tops that were no match when it came to hindering them.

"Michael is anyone likely to come along," gasped Corinne, beginning to feel his hardness growing as she was only wearing a flimsy pair of slacks. "No, no, that's not going to happen," he panted as he felt her probing hands feeling their way under his trousers and pants and onto his buttocks. With that he raised his body, so that he was now kneeling astride her and was tearing at his belt buckle to make his access a whole lot easier. Then he leaned forward and pulled down her skimpy slacks and flimsy underware.

With the rising scent from the now flattened myrtle berry bushes acting as an aphrodisiac, he lunged his way into her yielding softness. "Oh! Michael!" she gasped as quite miraculously and at their first attempt they both came together.

Luckily it was not far back down the track to their cars and thankfully there was still no one in the carpark to see what a state they were in. "I think we should go back to mine and dive in the shower," he suggested. Corinne willingly agreed, suddenly remembering that, thank God, she still had her overnight bag from staying with Alicia in the boot of her car where it had remained out of sight and luckily, out of mind.

His place, which she knew wasn't that far from Cheringford, turned out to be a three-bedroom house next to a wayside garage just beyond the small neighbouring village of Wixton. "Looks like you'd have no problems if ever your car won't start," she observed as she stood beside him at the front door while he fumbled with his key in the lock. "Bloody thing," he muttered almost under his breath.

"It's been playing up for weeks, but what with one thing and another I haven't gotten around to having it fixed."

Corinne shivered, suddenly feeling cold and uncomfortable in her damp and now green stained cream slacks. She looked around. The garage was closed and there was nobody about, but then mercifully, the lock yielded and they were inside the house, which felt warm and inviting. She followed him up to the family bathroom at the top of the stairs. "There's a shower over the bath; it's really powerful and set to a comfortable temperature," he said. "But what about you. Aren't you coming in?" He hesitated. "I have a small ensuite off my bedroom so I thought I'd use that," he admitted. "Come on don't be a spoilsport let's both use the bath," she invited.

Michael's home, she discovered, was tastefully decorated with fine quality furnishings and extremely neat, tidy and ordered.

Her initial impression from the outside had been of a rather shabby 1930s style house, probably built at the same time as the garage, but inside, it was little short of luxurious. The kitchen and dining room had been converted into one sizeable space and Corinne commented on the striking difference between the exterior and the interior of the property, while they were sitting at the kitchen table with two large mugs of tea. "Yes, I know. If this was my place, I wouldn't be leaving it in that state, but the garage owner, who lives in Cheringford, won't sell it to me and is happy to leave it just like it is." Later, curled up together on Michael's large sofa, Corinne started telling him about Lottie and Andy and his plans to take a sabbatical, so that he could further his career and gain more experience at some top award-winning restaurant in London.

"So, who's going to be running The Oreford's kitchen while he's away?" he asked. "That is yet to be decided, so might you with all your catering and hospitality industry contacts, have any suggestions?" she asked. "Well, what about me?" suggested Michael. "You?" replied Corinne, completely surprised by his out of the blue suggestion. "How could you possibly take on The Oreford with all your college commitments?" she pointed out.

"I actually think I've had about as much as I can take of running the catering department. It's not the teaching of the students, which I very much enjoy, but the increasing mountain of paperwork, the annual battle for my department's funding and all the college politics which go along with it, that's really beginning to get me down. So yes, if Andy does go off to town, then I'd be more than happy to step into his kitchen shoes," said Michael. Corinne thought about the implications of this for a few moments. "As manager, I'd sort of be your boss, which would be a bit weird don't you think?" He nodded in agreement, "But having said that, I just let Andy get on with his job and always have done," she told him.

"So, am I hired then? because I can't imagine having a nicer boss," he said, leaning over and kissing her. "I'm going to have to discuss this with my fellow family directors, but what would you do when Andy returns?" she asked. "I'll do what I have always done and let the future take care of itself, and besides, I'm not short of a bob or two which always helps I find."

Then her earlier vague thoughts of acquiring The Cheringford Arms popped back into her head and she began sharing them with him. "That would be a great project because, as you've already identified, the place is large, freehold, and bursting with possibilities. From what I know, the landlord and his wife have had the place forever and might well be ready to sell up at the right price." Michael asked if she would like to stay over, in which case he'd be delighted to cook her dinner. "I'd love to, but I really should go back as we have a busy night ahead," she replied.

Chapter 16

At that moment, Mark Hammond was purring slowly up Alicia's drive in a brand new, open top sports car and pulling up outside the house. Anthony, who was busy constructing a new den close by, heard the motor's distinctive engine note and came rushing across to greet him and enthuse over this magnificent piece of sports engineering. "Climb into the driving seat," Mark invited, and needing no further bidding, Anthony willingly took up the invitation, Alicia, alerted by the sound of the approaching motor, emerged onto the stone steps in front of the porch and was now looking down on them. They were like a couple of excited kids, she thought, her heart suddenly warming to the man who was making her beloved son so happy. That was a relief as over recent days, Anthony had become a little morose and she guessed he was beginning to grieve over the loss of his dad.

"It's quite all right to feel sad," she'd told him, putting protective arms around him. "I often feel sad too you know," she'd confided. But now somehow the unexpected appearance of a friendly face was cheering them both up. "Shall we take her for a quick spin and would mum like to come too?" he invited looking up and acknowledging her appearance. "Oh! can we Mum? Oh, do say yes," called Anthony, looking up at her from the driving seat.

"Yes, but only if there's room to fit Corina's car seat and Mark's got to promice not to go fast," she said.

Thirty minutes later they were motoring back towards Draymarket along the North Devon link road, having made their way out through the lanes to the nearest west bound access.

Mark had struck it lucky because the unexpected late afternoon outing, coming as it did at a time when both Alicia and her son were both feeling a bit down, had somehow turned a key in the unlocking of his way into their hearts.

He was invited in for a light supper, they'd had a cosy business chat over a couple of glasses of good red wine and he'd left with the lovely Alicia accepting his invitation to take her out to dinner.

"Isn't it about time you invited me back to yours?" was her parting shot, as he was climbing back into the car just as it was getting dark. Alicia wandered back into the house and up the stairs to say goodnight to Anthony, but his light was already off and he was fast asleep. Coming down again, she poured herself a glass of wine and began wondering just what she'd done. Although she'd had a lot of earlier reservations about Mark Hammond, she'd actually enjoyed his company, she decided.

Mark had always remained vague when it came to talking about his small North Devon estate, which even Royston had never visited, and therefore, Alicia had no idea what to expect when, three weeks later, he had picked her up and was driving her the last couple of miles through wooded lanes to The Manders.

Approaching an imposing pair of stone pillared, wrought iron entrance gates, Mark leaned his head out of his sports car and spoke a password into a small grey box positioned just at window level. Alicia watched intrigued as they slowly opened to reveal a drive leading through manicured lawns to a turning circle in front of a magnificent four storey Georgian mansion. Alicia thought her own home was quite grand, but The Manders was in a higher league altogether.

As they swept around the turning circle and came to a halt in front of the entrance steps, an elderly and slightly rotund man, wearing a dark suit, appeared at the porticoed front door.

"Welcome back sir and welcome to The Manders, madam," he said, stepping forward and taking the sleek brown leather laptop case, which Mark handed over to him to take into his study, overlooking the grounds at the back of the house.

It was indeed 'welcome back' because from landing at London City Airport on his inbound flight from Zurich, Mark had been chauffer driven to his exclusive club in the city where he had remained doing business for a couple of days before driving his new motor down to Draymarket to call on Alicia and then back up to town for a couple more weeks.

"What an amazing place," said Alicia, standing beside the car and gazing about her. On either side of the drive and set slightly back, were two giant and exotic hardwood trees looking as if they had stood there forever. "The previous owner, his father and grandfather, were all botanist, who travelled the world collecting specimens, many of which are to be found on the six acres of parkland, mainly at the back of the property," explained Mark, noticing she was taking an interest.

Alicia was given the grand tour, first around the ground floor with its large rooms and high feature plastered ceilings and into the massive kitchen with its giant oak table and state of the art oil-fired cooking range and then on into the sports and gun room containing all the equipment needed to stage shoot for up to twenty guests.

"I only acquired The Manders because it came with the opportunity of entertaining clients with a day's pheasant shooting out on the estate, which incidentally has proved extremely beneficial," explained Mark, leading the way back along the wide hallway towards the grand Georgian staircase.

"Who are all these fine ladies and gentlemen?" Alicia asked as, climbing the expensively carpeted stairs, she took in the faces gazing out from inside their heavily ornate gold frames on both sides of her. "I haven't got a clue, as I acquired them all from a stately homes death duties sale, but they do look rather splendid on my walls, don't you think?" came his surprise reply.

The first and second floors were lined with bedroom doors, as Alicia had expected, but Mark said he wouldn't show her into his master suite because there were some remedial works going on following a flood from a bathroom above. This was a lie as he did not think she was quite ready to be introduced to his series of highly erotic and provocative nudes that never ceased to arouse him when required.

It had been arranged she'd stay for a light supper before his chauffer drove her home, but towards the end of the meal, Anthony's friend Michael's mum called to say that Anthony was not feeling well and wanted to go home rather than staying for a sleepover. "Oh, dear I'm sorry Mark, but I'm afraid I'd better be going back now," Alicia apologised.

Disappointed, he watched as his Limousine disappeared down the drive, but never mind there were other distractions.

Entering his study, he switched on his wide screen television link with the strategically placed webcams around his penthouse in Zurich to see Chrissy and Jacob sitting in the lounge.

"Hello Mark, I wasn't expecting your call until much later tonight," she exclaimed with obvious pleasure in her voice.

It had been arranged that she'd stay in the penthouse with Jacob until she had secured her own place that he was to finance.

Chrissy had been given the largest of the three luxuriously furnished guest suits featuring a king size bed and large TV screen on the opposite wall. She was also surprised to find a further smaller camera screen strategically placed in the corner of the spacious ensuite wet room.

"I finished earlier than expected, so I thought I'd give you an early call to find out how the apartment hunting was going, but we can still talk later, say around ten," he replied.

"As a matter of fact, we've found a fully furnished apartment only about four blocks from here. It's much larger than I really need, but Jacob said he felt that would be OK with you," she told him.

"If Jacob thinks it's suitable, then it's fine by me," Mark replied amiably. "Oh, and Jacob will now give you one of our special debit cards, which will cover all your clothing and other shopping requirements and entitle you to draw Euros 6000 a month from today as your salary, so perhaps tomorrow, he should accompany you to our bank to set up a personal account," he suggested. "Mark that's so incredibly generous of you," replied Chrissy stunned by the amount she was to be paid.

"Don't thank me now because you can thank me later," said Mark, already beginning to feel aroused by the thought that, unless he was completely mistaken, he'd now bought her willing cooperation, mind, body and soul.

Nightcap in hand, Mark strolled into his bedroom, just after ten pm, and casually repositioned his webcam so that Chrissy would see him relaxing when he called her a few minutes later.

"Oh! there you are," she said catching sight of him, shirtless and sitting against his padded bedhead, as the screen in her room suddenly switched itself on. "Yes, here I am and feeling terribly frustrated at not being able to enfold your lovely lythe body into mine." Now she'd caught sight of the large erotic nude picture on the wall behind him and the penny dropped instantly.

"So would this help my sweet generous man?" she asked, slowly stripping off her top to reveal her perfectly formed breasts. Mark now instantly aroused, watched with wrapped attention, as she slowly and provocatively continued entertaining him.

Chapter 17

It was also being quite a memorable evening for Heather and Hannah Brooks, who were now entertaining Bob and Annie to supper. The foursome had spent the first part of the meal chatting about the effects Royston's tragic early death had had on everyone and how Alicia and Anthony were coping.

Bob said he was seeing a lot more of them these days, having accepted Alicia's invitation to take charge of maintaining Royston's car collection with Anthony's willing participation.

"There's a small fortune in that collection if she ever decided to sell it, but I guess that will never happen, seeing it's playing such an important part in Anthony's life," said Bob. "I can see it just remaining as a sort of permanent memorial to Royston's memory," he added.

"So, isn't it time we told Heather and Hannah our special news darling?" Annie suggested.

"I guess so, but you do it," he invited. She could see she now had their full attention. "Totally out of the blue, and completely unexpected, I'm six week's pregnant and our baby's due in mid-March," she announced. "And you are the first to hear," added Bob. "Wow that's amazing," said Hannah putting down her knife and fork and looking at them in disbelief. "No, not amazing, it's fantastic news," cut in Heather, "And that explains why you declined wine which had me thinking that perhaps, you weren't well," she laughed. "So, our heart-felt congratulations to you both," said Hannah, raising her glass in salute. "And one more thing," said Annie. "We want you both to be Godparents, but you won't know in advance if it's to be a boy or a girl because we've decided we're going to keep that a surprise until the birth."

Later, Bob began reminiscing about that first unforgettable late afternoon he and Annie had driven into Little Oreford acting as chauffer and companion to Charlie.

"I was your very first B&B guest that evening and by the end of the week you were treating me more like a brother," Bob reminded them, although, of course, they didn't need reminding. Then on a sombre note, they were remembering how the following evening they were all invited up to Royston and Alicia's for a barbecue. "I still can't really believe he's gone, even now," said Hannah.

Luke and Roxanne, had stayed on in Little Oreford for a couple of weeks and drove down to the coast most days to go surfing on Luke's favourite beach. Roxanne was new to the sport, but took to it like a natural and was soon riding the waves with growing confidence. But they never came away from the beach without collecting two large hessian sacks full of plastic waste, which came floating in on most every tide. The sacks were quite heavy and tended to become even more so when their bottoms became damp and sand encrusted. but Roxanne was adamant that using plastic ones would be a betrayal of their life-long eco mission.

Back at Albany House, Laura, who had far more free time on her hands than Ben, was continuously in operation wedding mode. She had already secured the appropriate size marquee, to come complete with quality green matting, internal heaters, especially as it was going to be October, and luxurious furnishings. These included a number of sofas, single armchairs and coffee tables for the large reception area just inside the entrance.

There was also to be a well-stocked complimentary bar area and a connecting catering tent, which was where her son-in-law Andy came in, having been charged to book the best outside catering company he could find. Next it was imperative to book St Michael's and the priest in charge, although Laura felt just a little hypocritical as the Jameson family never went anywhere near the church, except for Christmas carol services and occasionally to show the flag on Armistice Sunday. She knew one of the church wardens and it was from him she learned that The Rev Martin Clark was the leader of the local team ministry, based at St Andrew's in Draymarket. She left a telephone message which the vicar answered shortly afterwards, with an invitation for her to drop by for coffee the following morning around 11am.

Laura instantly recognised the Rev Clark as the vicar who had presided over Royston's funeral service and she had been particularly impressed by him at the time. He was about her own age with a boyish face and a most engaging manner, which she found attractive.

"Now correct me if I'm wrong Mrs Jameson, but I think it was your grandfather, the Rev Will Potter, who was rector at St Michael's for well over thirty years," he said.

"Yes, that's right and my mother is still living close by at Little Oreford Court."

The Rev Clark consulted his diary and said that 'yes,' he was free on the second Saturday in October and would be delighted to take the service and see the centuries old church packed for a change. "The trouble is, my congregation there has dwindled to less than twenty for my Sunday morning services and, apart from the

occasional funeral, that magnificent 13th Century building with so many fine architectural features, remains empty."
 Its upkeep was literally soaking up steadily decreasing resources, he explained. "Unless something can be done, I suspect we may have to seek to close St Michael's permanently in the not too distant future and once that happens, then I suspect it will never reopen again," he revealed.

The news that little Oreford was highly likely to lose its place of worship, which her grandfather and grandmother had spent virtually their whole lives cherishing, was a shock and suddenly too awful to contemplate. "Tell me, roughly how much you think you need a month to keep the church maintained and open?" she asked. It was the question he'd just hoped she would ask, having already calculated that if anyone was going to assist him in his mission to save St Michael's, it would be the late Will Potter's family. He already knew, from what he'd heard on the parish's now wilting grapevine, that the Jamesons were a family of some substance, already owning the popular Oreford Inn and the Old Mill House visitor attraction. "I think I could safely say that we need at least £3000 per month," he replied. At that moment, Laura was thinking of the mostly overgrown churchyard, where even the grass cutting had been restricted to a few yards either side of the main pathways, and of the awful state of her grandparents' and great aunt's graves, and was suddenly overwhelmed by a sense of guilt. "Well Martin, if I may use your Christian name, our family will take it upon ourselves to have the churchyard tidied up before the wedding and I am sure the donations made after the service will be substantial. I will then see just what can be done to ensure that our parish church remains open," she promised.

"Oh! Mrs Jameson that is most reassuring and bless you!" said the Rev Clark, already congratulating himself for a mission, hopefully accomplished, as he watched her walk down the vicarage drive to her car. 'Ask and you shall receive,' he said to himself as, putting his hands together, he looked up towards the heavens in the fervent belief that the good lord was listening.

Laura was pleased she had secured the vicar's services, but now also seized with a missionary's zeal to save her parish church. 'So, after our wedding, there could also be a christening in the New Year,' she mused, thinking ahead to the arrival of Annie and Bob's baby.

She found it mildly surprising that her mother never showed even the slightest interest in St Michael's where her father had ministered to his dwindling flock for so many years and where both her parents and sister were buried, but that was probably all tied up with her unhappy home life. Nevertheless, she was sure Charlie would write out a sizeable cheque to help save the church from closing. But Laura was not so sure it would be a good idea for the Jameson Family Trust to get involved, beyond hiring in gardening contractors from Draymarket to tidy up the churchyard. 'So, who else might she involve in such a church funding project?' she asked herself and then she thought of Alicia Randall's substantially wealthy friend Mark Hammond.

Chapter 18

The Oreford Inn was experiencing its busiest summer on record with the main bar, restaurant and large conservatory, now built out over part of the cobbled courtyard, full most every lunchtime.

There were now five satellite guest houses situated in the surrounding area, acquired by the Jameson Family Trust Fund and fitted out to a high standard, specifically to 'feed' customers into The Oreford. The strategy was working far better than Laura, Ben and Corinne had originally envisaged. Guests holidaying in the area were given discounts if they chose to dine at the inn during their stay and almost all took advantage of the incentive.

Annie was working more shifts than ever, coming in early to supervise check outs, going home to Little Oreford Court mid-morning and then returning to handle the bulk of the afternoon check ins. She was under strict instructions from Corinne not to overdo it, but insisted that being pregnant seemed to be agreeing with her because she was feeling really well.

Subsequently, with Corinne making a twice weekly round of the guest houses to ensure that their mostly young team of managers had everything under control and also being fully occupied running the former coaching inn, it was several weeks before she felt able to take a night off to catch up with Michael.

They'd talked on the phone most evenings during which they'd discussed the prospect of him taking over when Andy went off on his sabbatical, but now, she had some real news because. Luke's prospective father-in-law had been as good as his word and had secured an interview for Andy with Emile at his award- winning French restaurant the following Friday.

"So, I was wondering, as we are so busy at the moment, if you could possibly come in tomorrow and help him out and then take charge when he goes off for the interview. Lottie is going along too and they are going to make a long weekend of it, leaving the twins with mum, whose already enlisted Annie and Bob's support. So, as I'm going to be covering her shifts on reception, I'm going to be even more up against it and it would be so reassuring to know that things were under control in the kitchen," she told him. "Of course, I'd be delighted. It will be great to be back in my true working environment again, so let's celebrate with a glass of bubbly. You can relax and enjoy it while I start preparing supper," he said. Five minutes later he came back into the lounge with a platter of canapes as their starter.

"Believe it or not, when I was on the cruise ships, I had one chef who spent her entire working day just making thousands of these tasty savoury morsels. They were delivered fresh every afternoon at around 4pm to hundreds of guests occupying the more expensive state rooms, plus they were also served at all the numerous cocktail parties," he explained. "Didn't she find that all too much after a while," she asked. "Not really because she loved her savouries and was always coming up with new variations, and besides that, the task was a real challenge.

When you are catering for up to three thousand guests, plus around a thousand members of the ship's company, having your sixty-strong team of chefs concentrating on their individual specialities was the only way. For example, I had two chefs working all night in the bakery, another preparing and making every single dish involving potatoes and so on," he explained.

"And I've been going on about how busy I am when you had that vast catering operation to control day in and day out," laughed Corinne.

Over supper, she told him her other important news.

"Laura, Ben and I are having a meeting with mum, Robin and Margo tomorrow to consider the question of making a bid for the Cheringford Arms. If we do carry on with this project, it will pretty much clean out our £1.5 million Jameson Family Trust Fund which they only set up for us a couple of years ago," she revealed. "Do you think they will give you the go ahead?" he asked. "I'm not sure because before anything's decided, mum will most likely consult my stepson" James, whose an extremely wealthy Caribbean property developer, now based in the Dominican Republic, she told him. "You've never mentioned him before. Is there no end to the Jameson family connections?" Michael asked. "I guess the opportunity has never come up.

But you see, mum also once worked in the hotel business and met and married widowed Caribbean property developer, Hugo James, when she went out there to help open a hotel and golf complex. He had a seven-year-old son Jimmy, my stepbrother, who mum adored because they were both kindred spirits with adventurous personalities. Hugo sadly died of a heart attack in his early seventies and, as Jimmy had already taken over complete control of his father's business, mum decided to come home to live with a life-long friend in Sidmouth. They were together for ten years, and had whale of a time going off on cruises and lots of other holidays before she also died. It was then that mum moved into an expensive retirement hotel where Annie was the Duty Manager," she explained.

"It was from there that she decided to make a return visit to Little Oreford, where she'd grown up. And, as you already know, she discovered that Laura and I, the twins she'd given up for adoption, had both found our way back home," said Corinne.

"It's an amazing story, which I still find quite difficult to believe and would make a great 'wheel has turned full circle' theme for a novel," suggested Michael.

Not too many miles away as the crow flies, Alicia had bowed to the inevitable and had just served a simple supper of salmon fillets with a spicey stir fry to Mark Hammond as a thank you for his inviting her over. He had an overnight bag out in his car just in case the need might arise and felt the evening was going rather well. Anthony was up in his room excitedly getting to grips with a new Lego Technic model of a four-wheel-drive Land Rover Defender that Mark had brought him. He knew full well these kits cost way beyond his pocket money range, having gone online a number of times and lusted after them, and he also knew his mum would not have been overly happy had she known just how expensive this present was. Alicia had to admit she was enjoying their evening together, even so, she was still quietly determined to keep Mark as a friend.

Over the past few weeks, she'd definitely come to the conclusion she was rather enjoying having her freedom back again after so many years and it was going to be quite some time before she ventured into another long-term relationship. But as the evening wore on, Mark showed no signs of leaving and the more he talked about his world, the more anxious she became for him to leave.

Luckily, as she was about to say she felt it was time for him to go, there came a cry from upstairs. "Oh dear! Corina's been doing this quite often lately. It's as if she's been having some bad dreams and the trouble is, that once she wakes, it can take ages to settle her down again," said Alicia, getting to her feet from her end of the sofa. That was not quite true, but it had the desired effect on Mark, who also got to his feet, saying it was high time he was going anyway and that he would see himself out.

As it was, Corina settled back down in a couple of minutes and Alicia breathed a huge sigh of relief. "That was a close shave," she said to herself.

But Alicia's having to escape the attentions of admirers was not to be over quite yet because, around 11am the following morning, she answered the bell to find her former occasional lover, Peter, standing uncertainly on the doorstep.

"Peter what on earth are you doing here?" she asked, coming forward and giving him a brief almost impersonal hug before stepping aside to allow him to enter the hallway. "I thought it would be good to see you again, and as I've now moved to the West Country and taken up a new college post in Exeter, I thought it would be fun to drive across country and surprise you," he explained.

"You've certainly done that all right," she said, leading the way into the kitchen. There was a coolness in her attitude, which he detected immediately, and caused him to regret he'd made the journey. In his mind, he'd hoped she would welcome him with open arms for old and intimate time's sake, but this was not happening and he was beginning to feel highly embarrassed.

She was clearly now a woman of substance, so what could she possibly see in a middle-aged college history lecturer with hardly two pence to rub together? "I really shouldn't have come and invaded your privacy," he said, as she waved him to a stool next to the breakfast bar. "Well now you are here, you must stay for lunch, so that we can have a good catch-up chat," she said.

Peter left around 3pm and she stood on the steps and watched him drive slowly away in a car that had seen far better days.

Chapter 19

With her new Swiss bank account, six thousand euros salary, and a spacious, luxuriously furnished apartment, Chrissy Morales decided she was doing rather well. But then a small cloud appeared on her horizon when Jacob turned up with a TV engineer and several heavy boxes, which he'd wheeled out of the lift on a sack truck and were now sitting outside her door when she opened it. She made him a coffee while the operative went to work installing the large web cam screens in her lounge and master bedroom. "So, I guess I'm probably not the first to receive this lavish attention from Mark," she remarked as the prospect of having no escape from her boss's prying and lustful eyes, slowly dawned on her. "No, but not for quite a while and the others were not treated anything like as generously as you," he replied after a few moments "So what happened to them?" Jacob took another sip of his coffee and she could see, he was considering his reply. "There have been three of them, all professional women like you, whom he met during the course of his business and were swept away by his charm and wealth and promises of taking them onboard, but they all drifted back to their past lives, when they eventually realised there really was no future with him," said Jacob quietly. "As I suspected, but it's interesting that I've been singled out for some special attention, so maybe that's a sign that he really does intend keeping his promise and involving me in his affairs," she suggested.

"I think you'll just have to wait and see on that one, but I do have a proposal of my own that might interest you," he said now finishing up his coffee.

"Would you like another?" she asked. "Yes, why not, that would be nice," he said, watching as she took both their mugs and advanced on the coffee percolator. "So, what do you have in mind Jacob?" she asked as she stood pouring the coffee with her back to him. She was a fine woman, but then again, he was a now a confirmed bachelor, almost old enough to be her father. "As you are keen to get involved with the investment world, why don't you come around a couple of times a week and we'll go into the boardroom, switch on the screens and you can watch as I do a little trading on my own account," he suggested.

"Does Mark know you do this?" she asked. "No, but the British have a saying, which he uses occasionally, which is: what the eye doesn't see, the heart doesn't grieve." It wasn't long before the engineer had finished and handed Chrissy a thick user's manual before departing. "Don't

worry about that because I can easily talk you through it," said Jacob, quickly spotting the frown on her face.
"OK, so I suppose you'd better do it now then," she replied.

Chrissy took herself out clothes shopping after lunch, having arranged to walk over to Mark's penthouse around ten the following morning. He hadn't been in touch for a couple of days, but as the webcams had now been installed, she suspected she would be 'seeing' him later that evening. Men were so predictable when it came to their lust, she thought.

But there was another matter that had started nagging quietly away at her since the whirlwind excitement of her new life had started blowing itself out and that was, what to do about her old life.

She'd vowed she was never going back, but now she was beginning to miss the warmth, colour and vibrance of Costa Rica. She already knew in her heart of hearts that this impersonal European city with all its fine buildings, could never be home. So she would return as soon as she'd amassed enough cash to keep her in some style for a considerable time. But first, she'd have to call her boss and resign and that was not going to be easy, knowing just how persuasive he could be. Mark did call, around midnight and just as she was about to switch off her reading lamp, now casting an intimate glow over her bedside scene. He apologised for leaving it so late, but he'd been delayed by an over running business dinner in town.

He had, in fact, not long returned from Alicia's and was sorely in need of a consolation prize. 'Here we go again,' thought Chrissy, whose attraction to Mark was now undergoing a subtle re-evaluation. Slowly raising herself and leaning back against her padded bed head, she revealed her body, naked above the waist and in all its curvaceous beauty. "So how have you spent your day?" he asked, ignoring her nakedness, for the moment at least. "Jacob turned up this morning with a TV engineer, who installed these camera screens, as you can see, and then I spent the afternoon out shopping. I also began thinking it would be nice to have the use of a small contract hire car and to do a little exploring while you're away, and talking of that, when will you be back as I am really keen to start earning my salary?" Both knew full well, but neither could voice the fact, that she'd already started earning it! "I should be back in a few days, but in the meantime, the car is a splendid idea, and I'll ask Jacob to sort it," he said.

She'd got her car, so now Mark needed a little reward, she decided, casually pulling back the rest of her bed covers and slowly coming up onto her knees. At some deeper level, she was really enjoying, tantalising him because it was giving her a power over him and compensating for her being used. He finally bid her goodnight around 1am and she set her alarm for 5am, which she knew would be just after ten am in San Jose. By then, her boss Carlos would probably have completed his morning briefing with her former close crime busting 'family' and be back behind his ridiculously large desk in his small office. That huge chunk of wood, which for some bizarre reason had captured his fancy, was a relic from colonial times and she was remembering the day she and her colleagues had struggled to carry it up from the ground floor because it was too large for the lift.

Carlos answered the phone at its second ring and she could sense the delight in his voice, the minute he knew it was her.

"Chrissy I was beginning to wonder just when we'd be hearing from you because it's several weeks since Gabriella returned and she appears to have gone to ground, so what's the news?"

It was her moment of truth and she could feel her strong resolve to resign, melting away. "The good news is that he's really taken to me and set me up in a nice apartment, but the not so good news is that he's keeping me at arm's length from all his business dealings at the moment and switches off the minute I go anywhere near the subject. So, I don't really think there's any point in my staying here much longer. But I'm accompanying him as his window dressing, to some big international business conference in a couple of weeks," she lied. "So, I guess it will be worth sticking around at least until after then." There was a long pause while he considered her suggestion. "OK let's do that then, but I don't suppose you know what's happened to Gabriella do you?" Chrissy said she had no idea and put the phone down, relieved that she'd so neatly crushed his expectations and given herself another breathing space. She'd leave it at least three weeks before getting in touch again and explaining that she'd failed to find anything remotely incriminating against Mark Hammond. But, by the way, she'd fallen for an American living in the adjoining apartment and was moving in with him so she was resigning and would not be coming back at least not for a while anyway.

Chapter 20

For Lottie and Andy, dining out in London with her older brother and his fiancé and then to spend the night back at her place was a unique experience. To start with, it felt really weird and quite liberating not to have the twins with them. They'd arrived at Roxanne's late on a Friday afternoon and were now out for supper at a small Italian restaurant just around the corner.

Andy had always got on well with Luke because their paths often crossed when he was back home and his brother-in-law had taught him to surf after he'd first got together with Lottie, although there had been little time for sport after their twins arrived. But for Andy and Lottie, spending some quality time with Luke and Roxanne was going to be a completely new experience and they'd viewed it with some trepidation on their drive up from North Devon. "I do hope they don't come on too hot and strong with all the climate change stuff," said Andy and Lottie thoroughly agreed.

It had been a particularly busy week for Andy, not only because the restaurant and conservatory had been full most lunchtimes and evenings, but because he'd also been showing the ropes to Michael, who at Corinne's suggestion, had driven over to assist. With them away on their long weekend, this was the perfect opportunity for Michael to be introduced to the business, she'd argued. It was clear to Andy within just a few minutes that Michael knew exactly what he was doing and was perfectly capable of taking over and running the kitchen operation. He'd suggested, showcasing a few of his own favourite dishes and for a brief moment, Andy had felt possessive over his kitchen.

The evening at the Italian bistro was going well, Luke and Roxanne having already decided not to come on too heavy over climate change, and it was not long before the conversation turned to the family. "It seems to me, if you don't mind me saying so, that the Jameson family have sort of established the beginnings of a dynasty in Little Oreford with you guys as the next generation," observed Roxanne, having just been told about The Cheringford Arms project, "I've never really thought of it like that, but I suppose you might be right," Lottie agreed. "Changing the subject, what are you two planning on doing after the wedding and are there likely to be any cousins for the twins coming along anytime soon?" Andy asked. "I think the jury's out on that at the moment," replied Roxanne. "As you know, Luke's between jobs after his research funded Antarctica project was wound up earlier in the year, while I, to be honest, have never really had a proper job since gaining my climatology degree," she asmitted. "When I left university, I was going to save the world, but after making dozens of abortive applications to research institutions and environmental consulting firms just to be taken on for unpaid work experience, I decided to simply go off and broaden my own experience," she explained. "How were you able to do that?" Lottie asked. "Dad agreed to fund me for a year, provided I compiled a definitive research programme, which involved going off around the world and visiting climate change hot spots and producing my own assessment reports, which I did. I flew first to the Maldives, whose very existence is being threatened by rising sea levels, and not long after I arrived, I got chatting with an American family, who were staying at my hotel on holiday," she told them.

"It turned out that the dad edited one of America's top cultural glossy magazines. So, when I explained what I was doing, he asked if I would be interested in sending him a monthly feature on the effects of climate change from wherever I was in the world and, provided the pieces were interesting, he would pay me three hundred dollars per article. I jumped at the opportunity, as you can imagine, because suddenly I had a real legitimate purpose for my entire trip," she explained. "That's amazing and really goes to show just what opportunities can be created if you take a chance and go out into the world," said Andy, smiling at Lottie, who at once saw the significance of the comment, given his interview at Emile's the following morning. "So what are you both planning on doing now?" Lottie asked. "Go on. You tell them Luke," said Roxanne. "Believe it or not, we've both enrolled on teacher training courses starting at a London college in the middle of September. With our climatology and geography degrees and all our supportive experience, we figure that it shouldn't be too difficult for one, or both of us, to obtain college lectureships, because, after all, if we want to influence future generations re the climate change debate, then what better way to start than in the classroom."

Andy returned from his interview with Emile, fired up with enthusiasm and with the news that he was to join his team at the end of October as a Chef de partie, responsible for food preparation as the kitchen's resident chef was about to go off on maternity leave.

On the Sunday they were all taken out for lunch by Roxanne's father, who chose another award-winning restaurant where again he appeared to be on close personal terms with the proprietor. Dr Flavell ordered the most expensive twelve course taster menu and delighted in asking Andy for his professional opinion on each of the dishes. At some point during the luncheon, the conversation turned to the forthcoming wedding and Roxanne revealed that Lottie and Andy's twins were going to carry her train. "It would be nice if there was also a flower girl, don't you think Roxanne?" her father suggested. The question took them all by surprise but then Lottie came up with the answer. "Our Aunt Corinne's best friend Alicia has a three-year-old, so I guess we could ask her, if you'd like that Roxanne," she suggested.

Chapter 21

It was the third Tuesday in September when Jonathan and Shaun next met up for lunch in the revolving restaurant at the top of Toronto's CN Tower. Their paths had not crossed since their last evening together in Jonathan's den, back in July, because Shaun had spent most of the summer transacting some business in Vancouver, where he had now set up a small satellite office and was employing an associate. He was pleased to hear that his buddy had finally come out of the depressive mood he had been in since breaking if off with Corinne and later dumping Gloria. "I took three weeks off and went up to the camp for some fishing and messing about in boats and struck up a casual friendship with an American woman, who was staying with some neighbours of mine. It was purely plutonic, but we passed a few pleasant evenings together and now I have a standing invitation to visit her in Connecticut if ever I happened to be down that way," he explained. "Well speaking of vacations, I'm about ready for one myself, so are you still up for a trip over to the UK and a return visit to your folks in Devon?" asked Shaun. Jonathan thought about it for a moment. "Why not, but I think it would be pushing it to stay at The Orerford Inn.

Maybe we could find somewhere close by and then drive over to The Oreford for lunch and to see how the land lies," he suggested. "OK so when should we go?" asked Shaun. "How about around the first or second week in October," Jonathan suggested, having consulted his diary.

"I'll book the flights and sort out the accommodation if you like," offered Shaun.

"The last time I took a flight, you'll remember, was when Corinne and I flew down to Costa Rica and recovered the deeds to my family real estate, which my grandfather Joe and his brother Frank had been duped into handing over to that crooked corporation, by my cousin Brad," Jonathan recalled.

"I wonder if they're still wielding their malign influence over the region," Shaun replied. "No, the whole corrupt edifice was brought crashing down by serious crime investigators a couple of years ago. It made a small splash in the overseas business section of the Star and I can't think why I never told you at the time," he said. "So was Corinne's father arrested?" Shaun asked.

"No and that was the irony not lost in the newspaper report because it was just after his funeral that the serious crime people swooped," he explained. "Did you tell Corinne that her father had died and that his whole crooked corporation had been busted?" Shaun asked. "I thought about it, but in the end, I never did because, if you remember, she was so disgusted by all that he stood for, that she never told him she was his daughter and when she got home, she told her sister and her mother that we'd never found out what had happened to him, so I decided she'd not want to know," he replied. "That Costa Rica trip, being hijacked and flown off to meet your father's nephew must have been one hell of a scary experience," Shaun responded.

"It certainly was, but probably the most frightening moment was the sunny morning we were sitting by our San Jose hotel pool, surrounded by people enjoying themselves, and were approached by a local serious crime squad detective.

He was accompanied by a woman colleague and they told us this Mafia style organisation was looking for us. Anyway, that's enough of all of that, so here's to spending a couple of October weeks on holiday in England," he said raising his wine glass in a toast. But as their departure date drew closer, Jonathan began having some serious misgivings about the trip. Shaun was clearly very keen to see Alicia again, even if she was married, but he was not so sure that just turning up and surprising Corinne was such a good idea after all.

He agonised over whether to call her in advance, but then what if she made it clear she would not see him, especially as Shaun had already booked and paid for the flights? No, he'd just have to throw caution to the wind and go with the flow.

Mark Hammond never did get back to Zurich that summer, for one business reason or another and former San Jose serious crime squad operative Chrissy Morales was no longer really bothered whether he did or not. She still had to keep him entertained two or three evenings a week, but now she had a substantial income, her car for getting out and about and, far more importantly, her regular stock market trading sessions with Jacob. What started off as a couple of mornings a week had been extended to several afternoons as well, with lunch in the apartment or out at a small restaurant close by. She and Jacob enjoyed one another's company, purely on a platonic basis, but what was far more important, under his guidance, she'd now grown her original six-thousand-euro salary tenfold. Mark was always full of apologies for not coming back when he called up and had mentioned several times that perhaps she could fly over and join him on his country estate. Chrissy never pressed him to keep his promise, but it had given her the perfect excuse for stringing along her boss back in San Jose. Mark, she told him, had pulled out of that fictitious business conference at the eleventh hour, but now there was the prospect of her flying over to the UK to join him on his private estate, so he'd agreed that she should stick with it for a little while longer, because, at the end of the day, it would be well worth it if he could bring his quarry crashing down.

Mark was now spending much of his time at his London apartment overlooking the Thames, or around at his club, and was taking more than a passing interest in the Royston Randall estate agency chain, which gave him the perfect opportunity for keeping his one and only minority shareholder personally informed when he was down. He'd got into the habit of dropping by unannounced, which Alicia came to tacitly accept as being within her self-imposed boundary of maintaining a friendship and nothing more.

William Weaver, whom he'd appointed as the agency's Managing Director and given carte blanche to expand this off-shoot business, was it seemed, doing rather well as Royston had always assumed he would. "To tell you the truth Alicia, I am beginning to feel that I have more than benefitted from my buy-out arrangement with Royston," he confided on his latest visit to The Woodlands. "So, I am minded to increase your shareholding from ten to twenty per cent as some recompense," he announced, while they were sitting on the patio with a pot of coffee. "That would be extremely generous of you Mark, but as I don't really need the money, perhaps you might make a suitable donation to our local hospice," she suggested.

"They are struggling a bit at the moment and need all the financial help they can get," she told him. While Mark was perfectly happy to increase his investment in, and possibly influence over, Alicia Randall, he was not at all sure he wanted to support the hospice, however much of a worthy cause it might be. "Before I leave, I must ask if you happen to be free the second weekend in October to help me host some business associates, who are coming down to The Manders?" he asked, neatly changing the subject. "Oh no, I'm sorry because I'm tied up that weekend." she replied.

Mark drove away empty-handed yet again and feeling she was deliberately keeping him at arm's length. She'd rejected, more or less out of hand, his more than generous offer to substantially increase her holding in the estate agency and had then thrown him over in favour of some other engagement. But there was another reason why he had driven over to Draymarket, and that was to call in at the Gazette offices for a catch-up with his fellow trustee Jackie Benson. The newspaper's weekly sales were holding up quite well, she told him, and as Olly, her trainee, had now passed his exams and was willing to stay on, she was thinking of employing him. But that would mean an increase in the paper's wages bill, she pointed out. Jackie also wanted to take on someone to concentrate on selling space for the Gazette's online edition, which, she admitted, could do a whole lot better, given more time and effort, so as her fellow trustee, what did Mark think? "Will the generated income from more online advertising support the extra personnel?" he asked.

"Not in the short term, but as I am confident it will within six months," she told him.

I was thinking of calling a meeting with our three fellow trustees and seeking their support for my dipping into our quite substantial reserves," she confided. Mark said she could count on his vote and suggested they adjourn across the road to The Carpenters for a spot of lunch. It was during the course of the meal that Mark learned of the Jameson family's forthcoming wedding, which to all accounts, was going to be quite a grand affair with a service in the church and a marquee on the lawn behind Albany House. "I only know about it because they've hired Danny Williams, Draycott's professional photographer, who also freelances for us," she explained. "When is the wedding, Jackie?" Mark asked. "It's the second Saturday in October, which reminds me that I should really contact the family sooner rather than later re a wedding report," she added.

So that was why Alicia had turned him down out of hand instead of inviting him to accompany her, Mark thought as he drove away. But then again, why would she have invited him, when he'd told her he was hosting colleagues that weekend, he reasoned. All in all, it wasn't a very satisfactory situation because somehow, he had the unerring feeling she was never going to invite him to accompany her, whatever the circumstances had been.

Chapter 22

Corinne and Michael had fallen into a comfortable regime during the remainder of that busy summer. Not long after Andy and Lottie had returned from their London weekend, he'd asked Michael if he would now be happy to come in a couple of days a week to help out in the kitchen. "It's his depth of experience that I am still lacking and I am really enjoying benefitting from his support, and besides that, it's allowing me to spend a little more time helping Lottie with the twins," he'd told Corinne after the two had been working together for a few weeks. It was also the perfect arrangement from Corinne and Michael's point of view because the days he was over assisting Andy, he was also staying over with her.

"When Jonathan dumped me, I felt the bottom had fallen out of my entire world, but now I honestly don't think I have ever felt happier," she confided as they lay snug and warm together after making love. "I seem to have been a bit of a wanderer while looking for a soul mate all my life and now I've found you," he replied tenderly. "You said you felt like it was the end of your world when Jonathan ended your relationship, but it really is quite surprising how many times in life, something unwanted happens which, in fact, turns out to have done you a huge favour," he pointed out. "That's certainly true," agreed Corinne, turning over and switching off her bedside lamp.

It was also during that period, that Robin and Margo drove over to Little Oreford Court for one of their regular lunches with Charlie.

"Corinne and her Michael popped in for tea yesterday and he told me he was really interested in investing £250,000 in the Cheringford Arms project," she said. "It seems he has the cash from a previous house sale, but he's getting such a poor return on his present investment that he thinks he'd do far better to have a stake in The Cheringford, especially if he was able to oversee the refurbishment and then go on to run the business," she added. "This sounds like the perfect arrangement to me," said Robin, and Margo agreed.

The Old Mill House Visitors' Centre and Craft Workshops, were also having their busiest summer on record with the result that Ben was kept busy all day, every day and was having to leave virtually all the wedding preparations to Laura, who was in her element, and really enjoying the challenge. "My biggest worry, at the moment, is finding enough parking space around the village for everyone, because over forty of Luke and

Roxanne's friends have already confirmed they're coming," she told Robin and Margo. She and Ben were over at theirs for a Monday evening supper, a custom the four had observed for many years.

"There's one solution that springs to mind and that is we ask the Yardley Upton and Little Oreford Parish Council if we could use part of the village green because the ground's rock hard at the moment, so we wouldn't be doing much, if any, damage," suggested Robin. "Why didn't I think of that! So, do you think they would agree?" she asked. "We won't know until I ask them," he replied. "So more importantly, has Roxanne chosen her dress yet?" asked Margo. "Yes, she and her father spent most of last weekend looking at dresses and she eventually found one she liked, although Luke was not allowed to accompany them," said Laura.

"She wants it to be a surprise, but Albert has shared the secret with me," she revealed. "My wife's been spending quite lot of time on the phone to Roxanne's father of late and I'm beginning to feel quite left out," complained Ben, but no one took him seriously. "What's the dress like?" pressed Margo.

"Apparently, it's quite traditional and it really suits her, according to Albert, but we really must keep that to ourselves," said Laura.

"So, are you beginning to see the light at the end of the tunnel as far as all the preparations are concerned?" asked Robin.

"I'd say that Albert and I, with Luke, Roxanne and Corinne's help, are now almost there," said Laura. "We've eighty guests coming, the marquee company and the caterers are booked, and the luncheon and evening do menus agreed. The band from Draycott, whom we've used on previous occasions, will be playing during the afternoon and evening and we've hired a magician to circulate and help keep everyone amused," she explained. "You say there are over forty of Luke and Roxanne's friends coming, so where are they all going to stay?" asked Robin. "That's where Corinne has been an absolute star because she's taken that task completely out of my hands and sorted it," said Laura. "The minute we had the wedding date, she stopped taking anymore bookings for The Oreford and our five guest houses, with the annoying exception of one overseas reservation already in place at Rose Cottage. "We've found enough space for Albert and Roxanne and their immediate family at The Oreford and in our guest houses, with the remainder of Luke and Roxanne's friends booked into the travel lodge in Draymarket," she told them. "So, here's to the big day," said Robin, having just recharged their wine glasses.

Laura had meant to thank Robin and Margo for insisting on paying half the contracting cost of the major tidy up of the overgrown churchyard because, what with one thing and another, it had gone completely out of her head. But that, and perhaps with hindsight, her reckless offer to raise funds for St Michael's to prevent it from closing, did come firmly back into her mind two mornings later. It was while she was walking across to the church for a wedding planning meeting with the Rev Clark and the Draymarket florist, who would be preparing and displaying all the floral arrangements and decorations.

Chapter 23

It niggled away at Mark Hammond that he was clearly never going to form more than a superficial relationship with Alicia Randall, whatever he did, despite all his wealth and influence.

It made him feel unempowered and the more it gnawed away at him in his quieter moments, the more determined he became to punish her in some way, but in what way? that was the question. Then right out of the blue, the answer came in a surprise call from Laura Jameson, the proud mother of the groom in the forthcoming wedding of the year, as far as Jackie Benson was concerned. She was terribly sorry to trouble him, but she'd been given his number by Jackie Benson at the Gazette, who'd called to discuss a wedding report. Mark's heart began beating in anticipation of he knew not what. "The thing is Mr Hammond, I am raising funds to save our St Michael's Church here in Little Oreford from having to close and I am just wondering if you might be in a position to make a donation," she said, driving straight to the point. "How much do you think you need Mrs Jameson," he asked. "Our rector, the Rev Clark, thinks we need around £36,000 a year," she replied. Laura waited for his answer with baited breath.

"According to my diary, I am going to be back on my estate in North Devon on the second Saturday in October and I could drive over then with a view to meeting your first year's financial requirements." he offered. It was a master stroke and he knew it. Laura could hardly believe what she was hearing. "We do have my son's wedding on that day, but I don't suppose you would want to come along as our guest, would you?" she asked. It was music to his ears!

"My dear Mrs Jameson, a country wedding, how wonderful. I would be delighted to accept your kind invitation, if my partner could accompany me." Laura said that, of course his partner would also be most welcome, and she would be happy to send him an invitation, if he would kindly let her have his contact details. Mark was smugly satisfied. He could now turn up at the wedding with a stunning young woman on his arm and put Alicia 'snooty' Randall firmly in her place. His regular evening call to Chrissy came through an hour earlier than she'd expected and that was not the only surprise, because it seemed he was now going to make good on his promise of inviting her over to the UK to accompany him to a wedding. Jacob would provide her with a British Airways business class ticket and a car would pick her up once she'd cleared immigration at

Heathrow. But he would not be sending his private jet for her and that was a disappointment, for which he would have to be punished, she decided, claiming a blinding headache and a need for an early night.

Chrissy's earlier romantic feelings for Mark, following the realisation that she was never ever going to be more than a kept woman, had now evaporated. She was not at all sure she wanted to fly to England and attend a wedding on his arm and as his window dressing, but if she refused then she might be dismissed from his employment and she was not quite financially ready for that, not quite yet.

It was one of those sheer coincidences, that while her British Airways jet was depositing its passenger at the airline's Terminal Five, an Air Canada flight inbound from Toronto was arriving at Terminal Two.

Chrissy had found her business class seat far more preferable to the lesser comfort she'd enjoyed in economy on her Avianca flight with Gabriella from San Jose to Zurich, but Mark had not allowed her to fly first class and that had also annoyed her.

"Am I behaving like a spoilt brat?" she asked herself. The answer was surely 'yes,' but despite all his early promises to involve her in his business, a role she would really have relished, he had demoted her to that of a high-class prostitute after initially sucking her in with false promises as he had done with all others before her.

"Well, here we are in the UK at last," remarked Jonathan as they wheeled their trollies out into the main Arrivals Hall. It gave him an odd feeling of deja vu to think it was only a couple of years earlier he'd been making the self-same journey to meet Corinne waiting for him with open arms, but who could tell what sort of reception he was going to have this time around. He tried to push the uncomfortable thought out of his mind as they went in search of the nearest hire car desk. It was now too late to drive all the way to North Devon, so they'd decided to break their journey by stopping off along the M4 at The Marriott in Swindon, being a world-wide brand that was already familiar to them.

Over supper, Jonathan again agonised over whether to call up Corinne and break the news that he and Shaun were on their way to Little Oreford, but again he decided against it.

They left early and made a sight-seeing stop in the historic maritime city of Bristol to visit the SS Great Britain, the world's first iron trans-Atlantic passenger ship.

Jonathan had fond memories of the day he and Corinne had enjoyed a tour around the city with its famous Clifton

Suspension Bridge and Cabot Tower commemorating John Cabot's historic voyage to the New World. Taking Shaun to the top of the tower, he explained how it was from there, back in the 1960s, that Corinne's mother Charlie had begun her student freelance tour guiding activities that had resulted in her meeting and being left pregnant with twins by one Brad Meyer from Toronto. They left the city early afternoon and eventually turned up at Rose Cottage, between Hampton Green and Little Oreford, around seven. Being a Friday night, the young woman who booked them in and did not look at all well, said there would be no reservations available at the nearby Oreford Inn in Little Oreford because there was a wedding on. But that they'd be unlucky not to find a table at The Lion, just down the road in Hampton Green. Jonathan knew that anyway, having eaten in the pub with Corinne on several occasions, but chose not to mention it. "I can see why you found North Devon so attractive," said Shaun, once they were seated in the bar surrounded by a noisy bunch of Friday night regulars. "So, is it far to Alicia's from here?" It was the first time since they'd set out from home that he'd ventured to mention her name. "No, I'd say Draymarket is probably about five miles away," Jonathan replied. They got back to Rose Cottage about nine and spent a couple of amusing and interesting hours watching English TV, including the ten o'clock news, which Shaun observed had carried a report from Washington, but nothing from Canada. "To tell you the truth Shaun, I've watched quite a bit of British TV while staying with Corinne," said Jonathan.

"But while there are regular news items from the US, Canada's hardly ever mentioned." They decided they'd make a little tour around the area the following morning and turn up at The Oreford in time for lunch when who could possibly know what might be in store.

Chapter 24

While Jonathan and Shaun were enjoying their meal at The Lion, Laura, and Corinne were hosting Dr Albert Flavell and two close friends at a pre wedding supper in The Oreford's restaurant. Andy in his chef's whites had already been out to say hello prior to their orders being taken, while Michael, who was also busy in the kitchen, would be coming out to join them for coffee at the close of service. Roxanne and her two bridesmaids were staying over in the guest suites at Little Orford Court, where they were being entertained by Charlie, now in her absolute element, and by Annie and Bob. Meanwhile, Ben had taken Luke and his best man and two other friends over to The Carpenters in Draymarket for his stag evening, before coming back to spend the night at Albany House.

It was just after 6am that the sudden ringing of the phone beside her bed, dragged Corinne from a deep sleep. It was Juliette, her young manager calling from Rose Cottage. "I'm terribly sorry to call you Miss Potter, today of all days, but I feel so ill, I don't think I can even get out of bed, so someone's going to have to come over and prepare breakfast for our two American guests. I think I've probably got the flu which, I've been trying to fight off for a couple of days," she explained. "OK I'll be over right away, so stay in bed and I'll pop in to see you later," she instructed. "What a stupid girl. Why on earth hadn't she reported in sick rather than gone on spreading her infection around?" Corinne muttered as she hurriedly dressed. Thank goodness she only had two people to prepare breakfast for, she thought as she grabbed the spare Rose Cottage front door key from the small box by reception.

It was just after eight am when Jonathan and Shaun came down and entered the large and now sunny breakfast room and made their way to the table by the window, which had been set for two. "Looks like we're the only guests," remarked Shaun, hovering over the help yourself bar and pouring out two orange juices. Hearing their movements, Corinne, who'd already made all her initial cooked breakfast preparations, put down her mug of coffee, picked up her notepad and pencil and pushed open the swing door into the breakfast room. Jonathan and Shaun, now sitting at their table with bowls of cereal, looked up expectantly as she entered. There followed a stunned silence! "What on earth are you two doing here?" she uttered. "We thought we'd have a holiday and come over to see you and Alicia," replied Shaun, lamely, feeling like a schoolboy caught in the act of some crime and now in serious trouble. Corinne sat down at an empty table opposite and just looked at them, seized by a whole maelstrom of conflicting emotions.

"Why on earth didn't you let me know you were coming, rather than just turning up completely out of the blue like this?" she asked. "We were going to call later today to ask if you and Alicia would like to see us, but how could we possibly have known you'd be here?" said Jonathan. It was a fair point, she conceded to herself. "Well, you could not have chosen a more awkward day if you'd really tried because my nephew Luke is getting married in our village church at noon and I'm only here because our manager called in sick," she explained. "Oh my God. Look, just go back to The Oreford because Shaun and I can see to ourselves and we can catch up tomorrow or whenever," pleaded Jonathan.

Corinne faltered. "No, breakfast is already prepared, so we can all sit down and have it together and have a quick catch up, because if I don't have something to eat now, it simply won't happen." Jonathan now knew that he wanted to be with Corinne more than ever, but then his heart turned cold, as he suddenly spotted the tiny engagement ring that Michael had slipped on her willing finger the night before. He'd proposed in the few moments they'd spent together after the Flavell family party had all made their excuses and gone upstairs. It had been agreed it would be far more sensible for him to go back home and return to join Corinne at the church. It was while they were hugging and saying a brief goodnight, that he suddenly went down on one knee, took the tiny exquisite ring from his pocket and proposed. "I'm sorry but I couldn't wait a moment longer," he'd said.

Tearing his eyes away from Corinne's ring, which he could so easily have missed, Jonathan, was suddenly overcome by a terrible sadness and sense of loss, that she had now slipped beyond his reach forever. But it was all his own fault, so now all he could do was to try his utmost to rise above it, at least for now, if only for Shaun's sake. Out in the kitchen and cracking an extra egg into the frying pan, Corinne's emotions were also in turmoil. Oh, why, oh why did they turn up today of all days when Michael's engagement ring had only been on her finger for a few hours. She was pretty sure from the look on his face, that Jonathan had spotted it. Obviously, it had not worked out with that other woman so why on earth hadn't he told her. But having found Michael, would it have made any difference anyway? No, she simply could not bring herself to think about that, not now and not ever!

"So how is Alicia?" Shaun asked casually, once, Corinne had served their breakfast and they were all sitting awkwardly together, not quite knowing what to say to one another. It was the sixty-four thousand Canadian dollar question that had been burning a hole inside him ever since they'd agreed to come to the UK. It was the one question Corinne should have anticipated, but it still hit her like a shock wave. She hesitated. Surely it was for Alicia to explain that poor Royston had died, but not before she'd had a three-year-old daughter. If she broke the news right there and then, might not Shaun, quickly do the maths and begin to vaguely wonder if the child might be his! Then the answer came to her. "Look Jonathan, at the end of the day, you and I are still 'family,' and even though we're no longer together, I know everyone will be pleased to see you." She paused. "So, there's no reason why you should not both come to the wedding and all the afternoon and evening celebrations. I will tell Alicia you are here and I am sure she'll be very pleased to see you both. Her impromptu suggestion took them completely by surprise. "Are you really sure that would be all right and you'd be happy with that, even though we will not be suitably dressed for a wedding?" Jonathan asked. "That's where you are in luck because Luke and Roxanne have a lot of fairly alternative friends and the dress code is casual, so you'll probably be as well dressed as most of the guests with the exception of the close family, who will be formally attired. It so happened that two of our guests cancelled yesterday, because of illness, so there are places for you. But now I really must go and see how my manager is and then get back because I have so much to do before the wedding, which is at noon, by the way," she said.

Corinne's thoughts were in confusion as she drove home, having assured herself that her young manager would probably be OK after a couple of days in bed. Seeing Jonathan again had come as a complete shock, but no, her love for him had faded and she was going to be happy spending the rest of her life with her lovely Michael, she resolved. But she'd have to call him and tell him about Jonathan and also break the news to Alicia. However, both were preoccupied getting ready for the wedding and failed to pick up her calls. Jonathan debated whether or not to tell Shaun about his shock discovery, but decided against it, at least for the time being. But it hadn't escaped Shaun's notice that Corinne had made no reference to Royston when he asked about

Alicia, who was at that moment struggling to get herself, Anthony and Corina ready. Her son, looking extremely smart in his grey suit and blue tie, was not happy that his pleas to allow Michael to attend had fallen on deaf ears and was not being particularly helpful, which was not like him, but worst of all, Corina had suddenly taken against being a flower girl. Being entirely on her own and having to dress for a wedding, while coping with two reluctant children with no one around to help on such an occasion, was trying to say the least.

Chapter 25

When Chrissy came out into the Heathrow Terminal Five Arrivals Hall, she called up Mark, only to be told that something had come up requiring his attendance in town, so as he now needed his chauffer driven car, could she possibly jump into a taxi and give the driver the address he'd now text her? This was adding insult to injury, as far as Chrissy was concerned, and her mood did not improve, the nearer she got to The Manders. They had stopped at a busy and impersonal motorway service area, where she queued for the toilets and coffee and, worst of all, when he did return after his busy day, all he'd probably want to do was to relax, screw her and fall asleep in her arms. But her mood lightened as the electric gate opened and the car pulled up in front of Mark's magnificent Georgian Mansion and a slightly rotund and liveried butler came out to pay off the driver. "Welcome to The Manders Miss Perez," he said, picking up her two new, top of the range, travel bags, and ushering her inside.

Treating her with old world courtesy and charm, he ushered her into the drawing room with its plush furnishings and large widows looking out over green lawns. "Mr Hammond has asked that I make you feel

completely at home until his return, so might I start by asking if you would like to take afternoon tea," he asked.
"That would be good, but first I'd like to freshen up after my quite long and tiring journey," she told him.
She followed him up the wide staircase to the first level and he led the way along a corridor and into a magnificent suite overlooking the grounds.
He put her cases down and showed her its luxurious tiled bathroom before making his excuses and closing the door quietly behind him.
Before unpacking, Chrissy opened what looked like a connecting door to find herself poised on the threshold of Mark's bedroom. She recognised it immediately from its large and highly erotic nude portraits of both the male and female form. Suddenly the scene upset her and she turned around, closing the door behind her with the overpowering feeling that she wanted to be out of there and free of Mark Hammond as soon as was possible.
Standing looking out of the window and over the manicured gardens, she began calmly considering her options before changing into cream trousers and a blue silk top and going back down to the drawing room where a large pot of tea and plate of scones had been set on a table. "I'm so glad you've been making yourself at home

Angelina," Mark said on entering the room a few minutes later and embracing her.

Dinner for two was served by Frederick on the open balcony of a summerhouse attached to the main building by a glass panelled walkway and overlooking a small lake. "Now tell me all about this wedding we are attending," invited Chrissy. "Not really a lot to tell other than a lady called Laura Jameson, whose raising funds to save the church at Little Oreford from closing, asked me for a donation and I offered her £36,000, whereupon she invited me to her son's wedding there," he explained. "That was pretty generous of you," said Chrissy.

"Let's just say that she caught me at the right moment, but now I've something far more important to discuss with you," he said.

"The real reason for inviting you over was to ask if you'd stay on and manage this place for me because I'm spending more time here now and less in Zurich where you must admit Jacob has pretty much everything under control. 'He sure did,' she thought, remembering all the companiable afternoons they spent using his system to make themselves rich. "What would my duties be?" she asked, wanting to add: Apart from the obvious ones that is.

"Everything really from running the estate and keeping my diary through to helping me host events, especially in the pheasant shooting season, he replied. "So, who handles things now?" she asked. "I have an estate manager in charge of the grounds and the shooting and will go on doing so, and Frederick who looks after the house and my engagements, with the help of a part-time secretary. But Frederick's coming up for retirement and I have to make alternative arrangements, so naturally I thought of you." There was a time early on in their relationship when Chrissy would have jumped at the opportunity, but as the weeks had passed, she'd realised that he'd always remain detached and aloof and was never going to be her confidant or soul mate. Now he was asking her to be nothing more than a glorified housekeeper and otherwise kept woman. She'd already saved enough cash, so all she really wanted to do now was to escape back to her beloved Costa Rica and resign from the Serious Crime Squad. "Now that is something to think about," she replied. Not long afterwards, they retired to his suite where the remainder of the evening played out very much as Chrissy had predicted.

They rose around nine, after a final love-making session. Mark looked on approvingly as she tried on the three smart outfits he'd instructed her to buy in preparation for the wedding and he chose the one he considered the most stunning and likely to impress Alicia Randall. By eleven, they had climbed into his magnificent blue top of the range sports car and were driving through sunlit and leafy lanes on their way to Little Oreford. Unknown to Mark, her designer Italian leather clutch bag contained her passport, a little English cash, her Swiss Bank account debit card and a small item of personal insurance.

They were there because Chrissy Morales had made up her mind that, whatever happened, she would not be returning to The Manders with this user of a man.

Corinne got back to The Oreford just as the Flavell family party were finishing breakfast in the otherwise empty restaurant. Making sure they had all they wanted, she went up to her apartment to bathe and changed into her wedding outfit before walking over to Albany House to join Laura and Ben.

Roxanne and her two bridesmaids were all getting ready at Little Oreford Court, attended by a local hairdresser and make-up artist and helped by Annie and Lottie, whose twins were jumping around and getting in everyone's way until Charlie took them off to calm them down and read them a story. Bob was outside giving his white ribbon-bedecked Bentley a final polish before driving the bride and her bridesmaids over to St Michael's, with the rest of the family following on in Lottie and Annie's cars.

As things worked out, there were a couple of last-minute hitches with the final wedding preparations, meaning that Corinne ended up hurrying into the church just ahead of the bride and her father. She'd not had a moment to break the news to Alicia about Shaun and Jonathan. Michael, who was already in his seat, reached out to squeeze her hand and was surprised to find she was no longer wearing his ring. "That must be the shortest engagement ever," he whispered in her ear, "I've taken it off because I don't want anyone seeing it and congratulating us when this really is Luke and Roxanne's day," she whispered back. "You think of everything my love," he said giving her hand another gentle squeeze. Jonathan and Shaun spotted a convenient layby just before Little Oreford and decided to walk the last hundred yards to the church and time their arrival so that they could sneak in and stand at the back just before the service began.

St Michael's was packed because most of the Jameson's village friends and neighbours had taken up their open invitation to come along to the service. Standing next to Jonathan and Shaun was Councillor Wayne Sharp, the new and youngest ever chairman of Yardley Upton and Little Oreford Parish Council, who'd willingly agreed to the Jameson's request to reserve a section of the village green closest to the church as an overflow car park. He was accompanied by his wife Felicity, who was a potter and was on the waiting list for a studio at The Old Mill.

It soon became apparent to all that the Rev Martin Clark verged on the evangelical and the short service was joyous and full of interest, thanks to the long note taking session he'd had with Luke and Roxanne a couple of days earlier. He'd realised the couple were quite alternative in their outlook and were completely happy to let him take charge and make the service as joyous as possible.

The result was that he bussed over members of his gospel style choir to belt out the few hymns the young couple had chosen.

Service over, Luke attired in a smart light grey suit and matching tie, led Roxanne back down the aisle in her flowing white dress and train, which the twins had now abandoned, to the traditional wedding march, because on that, Dr Albert Flavell, backed up by Laura and Ben, had insisted. Being on the end of a row, which had eventually squeezed up to let them in, Jonathan and Shaun had a good view of the immediate family following on behind the newlyweds. Now Corinne was coming down the aisle towards them accompanied by a lean, blue suited man with a shock of blond hair and probably about Jonathan's own age. This was surely her fiancé and from the look on her face, she was happy.

Filled with regret and remorse, he looked away in order to avoid eye contact, which was now the very last thing he wanted and in doing so, missed seeing Alicia, who was following behind with Anthony and her three-year-old flower girl now in her arms.

But Shaun had not missed her and his heart leapt as she passed less than three feet away from him, but looking in the opposite direction. He nudged Jonathan. "Did you notice Alicia was on her own with her son and a child she must have had since we last saw her, but not with Royston?" he whispered, hardly managing to contain his rising hopes that she might now be free.

Jonathan, now experiencing the exact opposite mix of emotions, whispered back that he'd been looking the other way. But it did seem strange that Corinne had never mentioned that Alicia had had another child, unless of course, she belonged to a friend or relation. "There's probably a perfectly logical explanation why Royston isn't here," he added.

Most male heads had turned when the stunningly attractive Chrissy Morales had walked up the aisle on Mark's arm and now her striking looks were having a similar effect as the couple walked back towards the church porch. Once outside where everyone was milling about and chatting in the autumn sunshine, Mark suddenly decided they should walk over to the green and check that his motor was OK and that fellow guests had given it a wide and deferential berth. They'd only been back at the car for less than a minute when Chrissy became aware of a boy running excitedly towards them. "Hi Mark, you've brought the open top then." It was immediately clear to her that he knew Mark very well. "We didn't expect to see you here, did we Mum?" he said turning to a tall, slim woman with long ash blond hair who had followed her son over with a young child in her arms and was now looking uncertainly at them. "Can you come over again soon and take us out for another spin because the last one was so cool?" the boy urged. "Not now Anthony. How are you, Mark? I didn't know you were back in the country." It was clear to Chrissy

that he knew this woman very well indeed, and it was a relationship he'd certainly been keeping to himself.
"Hello Alicia. How nice to see you, so may I take this opportunity of introducing my partner, Angelina Perez. Angelina and I work together in my Zurich office and now she's flown over to assist me at The Manders." The confused look on Alicia's face told Chrissy that her sudden appearance on the scene had come as quite a shock.

It suddenly occurred to her with crystal clarity that perhaps, this calculating man had gone to all the expense of flying her over to the UK and deciding what dress she should wear to this wedding, simply to spite this unsuspecting woman, who'd probably displeased him in some way. Now it was obvious to Chrissy from the smirk on Mark's face, that her appearance on his arm had had the desired effect.

Alicia had succeeded in keeping Mark at arm's length and just as a friend, but in some perverse way she'd also missed his attention. Now here he was with a beautiful woman on his arm and here she was surrounded by all these happy couples and feeling quite alone. Of course, she'd fully supported Corinne's steadily developing relationship with Michael, but it still served to emphasize her growing sense of loneliness.

Mark having succeeded spectacularly in teaching Alicia a lesson had suddenly lost all interest in the wedding. "I think perhaps we'll not attend the luncheon, seeing that we are really outsiders and don't know anyone here," he said, as they watched Alicia and her small family walk away. This was all the confirmation Chrissy needed that her earlier assumption had been correct. "Won't that be rather rude Mark?" she pointed out. "With everything going on, the groom's mother's hardly likely to notice that we didn't stay and besides that, I'm not altogether happy about leaving the car here," he replied. "Well, you can go, but I am staying because I'm all dressed up for the occasion and I'll probably never have another opportunity to experience a traditional English wedding," she retorted. Mark could hardly believe what his ears were telling him.

"You aren't being serious," he replied. "Yes, I am being perfectly serious; you can drive on home and I'll get a cab back later," she told him. "If I drive away from here without you, you won't be welcome back," he warned, shocked that his authority was being directly challenged by this ungrateful woman. "Fair enough, then I won't come back," she said, turning and following the crocodile of people, heading across the green towards Albany House where the white canvass top of the marquee could be seen rising above the surrounding greenery. "Have it your own way," he muttered, climbing into his car and roaring away, safe in the knowledge that she would come crawling back because what else could she do? he reassured himself.

Chapter 26

Jonathan and Shaun followed the crowd towards the marquee, and hung back, when they saw the bride and groom and their immediate family, lined up in row to welcome their guests. Then they spotted Corinne and her man making their way towards them. "Jonathan and Shaun, I would like to introduce you to my fiancé Michael." Corinne was fairly confident her news would not come as a shock because she was sure Jonathan had spotted her engagement ring at breakfast, although he'd not mentioned it. Jonathan was the first to speak. "Michael you are a very lucky man, and I should know, and I do hope that we can go on to become good friends," he said extending his hand. "Jonathan, I do hope so," replied Michael, who hadn't had much time to recover since Corinne had told him the surprise news that her ex was attending the wedding. "Corinne have you by any chance told Alicia we're here?" Shaun asked. "I had meant to, but then I thought perhaps I should leave that to you," she replied.

"And I guess there's no time like the present, seeing that she and the children are just over there," she said nodding towards a large tree on the edge of the garden, where Anthony was idling on a swing, dangling from a long rope, fixed high in the branches. "I'll go over then," he said, leaving them and walking towards her with his heart thumping. Alicia was close to tears, going over that uncomfortable incident with Mark and suddenly feeling an incredible loneliness, heightened by the happy family scenes all around her. "A penny for your thoughts, or so you used to asked me," said an instantly recognisable voice and Alicia looked up to see Shaun standing there in front of them.

"Oh my God Shaun. Where on earth have you sprung from?" she uttered, her heart suddenly leaping for joy. "Jonathan and I felt in need of a holiday, so we thought it was high time we just jumped on a plane and came over to see you and Corinne," he explained. "Anthony and Corina say hello to one of mummy's very special friends," she said to her children. "So where's Royston?" he asked. A small cloud appeared on her previously radiant face. "Sadly, he suffered a massive stroke and we lost him back in April," she replied quietly. "Oh, Alicia I am so, so, sorry," he said, stepping forward and enfolding her in a gentle bear hug of an embrace It was all too much for Alicia, who began sobbing uncontrollably in his arms. "Oh! Shaun, you can't know just how surprised and pleased I am to see you," she, cried through her tears. "And me you," he replied, gently stroking the back of her neck. "Are you all right Mum?" asked Anthony, his voice full of concern. "Yes darling, of course I am," she said stepping back and drying her eyes with a small handkerchief she'd pulled out of her jacket pocket. "Pleased to meet you Anthony," said Shaun, formally shaking his hand. "And what a pretty flower girl you are," he said, instinctively sweeping Corina off her feet and holding her in his arms. To Alicia's amazement, her child, who should have let out a howl of protest at being suddenly picked up by a complete stranger, just snuggled into his arms. Could it be that at some instinctively deep level, her three-year-old knew he was her father? Alicia asked herself, now beginning to regain her composure. But when should she break the news to him?

True, she'd agonised about getting back in touch with Shaun, but not telling him that Corina was his child. But now faced with the reality, she could not wait to tell him when the right opportunity arose. Seeing that Alicia and Shaun had finished embracing, Corinne left Michael and Jonathan talking and went over to join them. "I'm sorry I didn't have time to tell you that Jonathan and Shaun were here before, but now I think we should all be going in. As you already know, we've had two last minute cancellations so Shaun, you and Jonathan are on the table at the far end," she said. Just a few yards away, Chrissy was hanging back uncertainly from the end of the now dwindling line of guests waiting their turn to enter the marquee, a totally alien and intimidating environment to her. Should she just turn around and walk away now? she agonised, Countless times she'd kept a cool head in dangerous situations, but this was something well outside her comfort zone! No that would be a cop out and copping out was something that Chrissy Morales just did not do, she told herself. 'Goodness who was this coming?' thought Laura, the first in line of the reception party. She could see the look of uncertainty on the face of this strikingly attractive and expensively dressed younger woman, as she held out her hand to welcome her. "I'm Laura, the groom's mother, but I don't believe we've met," she said. "No, I am Mark Hammond's partner, but unfortunately he's suddenly been called away by some business emergency," she lied. "I am sorry to hear that, but you are most welcome," Laura replied, wondering if that meant she could wave goodbye to the £36,000 donation he'd promised. Once thankfully inside, Chrissy, spotted the seating plan posted up on a board and quickly located her circular table set for twelve with most of the guests already in their places.

Again, she hovered uncertainly, wondering which seat to take until the youngish man closest to her suddenly saw her embarrassment and came to her rescue. "Hello I'm Wayne Sharp and this is my wife Felicity and I can see from the card next to me that you must be Miss Angelina Perez," he said, getting to his feet and making room for her to sit down. Chrissy thanked him and took her place, smiling around at all the other guests as she did so, while surprising herself by suddenly taking control of her situation, "Unfortunately, my partner, Mark Hammond, has been called away on business, but just to let you know, there is a small mistake on the name card in that my name is Chrissy and not Angelina," she explained.
"Well Chrissy sounds a lot nicer name to me," boomed a rotund and waist coated man to her left, who was clearly already well into party mode. "I'm Claude Eustace Long from just down the road in Yardley Upton and where are you from might I ask my dear?"
Chrissy smiled back, having taken an instant liking to Claude. "At the moment I live in Zurich," she replied. "Well, that sounds a lot more exciting than Yardley, I must say," he responded.
Out of the corner of her eye, Chrissy now spotted two good looking men, probably in their mid-forties, walking

purposely in their direction. "Ah our final table companions have arrived," declared Claude, the Jameson family's solicitor, who seemed to have taken charge as their Master of Ceremonies. Jonathan and Shaun took their places directly opposite Chrissy, apologising for their late arrival and introducing themselves. "We seem to have quite an international flavour to our table, seeing you are both from Toronto and Chrissy here hails from Zurich," said.

Now Chrissy was making friendly eye contact with Jonathan and Shaun and realising instantly that she had seen the older man somewhere before, but where and when, those were the questions. For senior serious crime agency operative, Chrissy Morales, had gained an enviable reputation among her colleagues for never forgetting a face when it came to trawling though pages and pages of suspects.

The round table chatter was temporarily suspended while The Rev Clark stood to give the blessing, but the minute it was over, Chrissy returned to surreptitiously studying Jonathan's face when she thought he wasn't looking, but then he caught her at it and returned an engaging smile. She was an extremely attractive woman and what was more, she appeared to be on her own, he noted hopefully. There was also something vaguely familiar about her but what? Perhaps she reminded him of some TV personality, because she certainly had the looks for that.

Sitting closest to the top table, Alicia and Corinne were deep in conversation about Shaun, while next to them, Michael and Andy were discussing alternative recipes for the starter that had just been placed in front of them.

"The question is whether or not I should invite them both back to mine tonight, or would that be insensitive as far as Jonathan is concerned, when Shaun and I will almost certainly end up in bed together?" said Alicia.

"And, more importantly, when should I tell him about Corina?" she asked. "Perhaps it might be best if you don't rush into anything quite yet and let them go back to Rose Cottage, at least for tonight," Corinne suggested.

"You are probably right," Alicia conceded.

With the main and sweet courses over, it was time for the speeches and, as expected, Dr Albert Flavell, the founder of the feast, was soon in full flow giving a fine performance full of anecdotes about his beloved daughter and jokes that appealed to his mostly younger audience and made the marquee rock with laughter. After overcoming some initial nerves and encouraged by his now increasingly vociferous audience, Luke managed to rise to the occasion, as did his best man with more jokes and stories. But all through the wedding breakfast, Chrissy continued trawling her memory banks for where exactly she had seen this very attractive older man, almost to the point that she was otherwise oblivious to all that was going on around her.

The same was true for Alicia, whose thoughts continued to be dominated by Shaun, except while standing for all the obligatory toasts and the moments when she was tending to the needs of Anthony and Corina sitting each side of her.

There was the traditional comfort break before coffee was served and when everyone on Chrissy's table had returned to their seats, Claude, now tired of speaking to those on either side of him and straining to hear the conversations of those on the opposite side of the table, suggested that everyone should swap places. Jonathan was quick off the mark and without making it too obvious, managed to slide himself in beside Chrissy, while Shaun after some initial confusion, ended up next to Claude. Gradually the tables were abandoned as the guests, including Corinne and Michael and Alicia and the children, began making their way back out into the sunshine and clustering in small happy, chattering groups.

But where were Shaun and Jonathan? Alicia kept asking herself as the minutes passed and she kept on scanning the gathering. They hadn't just left, had they? she wondered giving way to a momentary panic. Unable to stand not knowing a moment longer and leaving the children with Corinne and Michael, she hurried back into the marquee where a few guests were still standing about deep in conversation and the waitresses had begun clearing the tables. Then, thank goodness, she spotted them apparently deep in conversation with Mark's partner. So where was he and what on earth was going on? "Alicia, there you are," said Shaun, getting to his feet. "I should have come out ages ago. His welcoming voice instantly reassured her, but what were they doing with that woman! Chrissy's heart missed a beat as it was clear that both these charming men, to whom she had just so easily unburdened her embarrassing story, knew Mark's friend. Moments later, Alicia was seated next to Shaun while Chrissy retold how she'd fallen out with Mark and how he'd got angry and driven off without her. "So here I am, luckily with my passport, credit cards and some cash and absolutely no intention of ever going back to The Manders. But having said that, with nowhere to stay and only the clothes I am standing up in," she explained. "Don't worry about any of that," said Jonathan, now taking control of the situation. "We can easily find you somewhere to stay tonight, and luckily there's a shopping complex not far from here where you'll be able to find everything else you need." Alicia exchanged a knowing glance with Shaun because it was blatantly obvious that Jonathan was more than eager to play the knight in shining armour to this highly attractive damsel in distress and now, she was going to help things along.

"Look, most everyone will be drifting off home for a couple of hours and then returning for the evening party so Chrissy, why don't you come home with me and the children and we can all meet up again later," she suggested. " Are you sure?" asked Chrissy. "Of course, I'm sure, I have plenty of room and can easily put you up for the night," she said looking at Jonathan.

What she did not say was just how much she'd enjoy having the last laugh on Mark Hammond.

Chapter 27

Driving back to Draymarket with two tired children in the back of the roomy four-by-four she'd recently treated herself to on a spur of the moment visit to Hendon Motors on the edge of town, Alicia began telling Chrissy all about her life and how Mark Hammond fitted into the picture. She also told her briefly how she and Corinne had come to know Jonathan and Shaun and had spent a holiday with them at their homes in Toronto, but she steered well away from any of the romantic and personal details.

When asked how she'd come to know Mark, Chrissy told her original cover story, more or less as it was, but with no mention of Jacob or the other covert details, or of her crime operative's badge, still hidden neatly in a side pocket of her designer clutch bag. "I know this will sound ridiculous Alicia, but I have a strong feeling I have met Jonathan somewhere before, although given that he lives in Toronto, I can't think how that can be at all possible," she confided.

At more or less the same time, Jonathan and Shaun were on the short drive back to Rose Cottage, both elated for different reasons. "I think this is being one of the most incredible days of my life, old buddy," said

Shaun. "How could we possibly have imagined, or even made up, the sequence of events that have unfolded since we entered that breakfast room this morning?" Jonathan could only agree.

Charlie walked back across the green with Robin and Margo and went in for a cuppa and a chat about all the exciting happenings of the day.

"I was right that Luke would somehow manage to bring the climate change debate into his speech, seeing that so many of their close friends share their views," said Margo. "Do you know sister, it doesn't seem five minutes ago since that, never to be forgotten, afternoon when we invited Laura and Ben and the children around to give them the keys to Albany House and I switched on the TV to see pictures of a forest fire. I suppose Luke must have only been about eleven at the time and when I explained that the fires were probably the result of climate change and what that was, he surprised me by saying he'd become a climate change scientist when he grew up," he told them. "Yes, it's funny how moments like that, stick in one's mind," agreed Charlie. Bob called in a few minutes later to collect her. "Oh! you've removed all the ribbons. I'd rather hoped you'd have left them on for our ride home." Bob smiled to himself because that was Charlie all over.

Heather and Hannah, who'd already had far too much of Albert's fine quality Champagne, were not going home because what was the point? Instead, they retired to The Oreford where they were soon having a riotous time in the bar with a group of Luke and Roxanne's young friends, already in evening party mode.

Across the courtyard and up in Corinne's apartment, she and Michael had taken off their smart wedding attire and were resting on the bed. "It must have been quite a shock to enter the breakfast room at Rose Cottage and find Jonathan and Shaun sitting there," he said. "Shock, that has to be an understatement," said Corinne. "When I'd got over my initial surprise, I can't say I was sorry to see them because I had been in love with Jonathan and I'm also very fond of Shaun. But thank goodness you slipped your ring onto my finger last night because the minute he spotted it, he knew without any words needing to be said, that our time together was really over," she revealed. "I'm glad I proposed too and seeing that you have raised the subject when do you think we might get married?" She knew it was intended as a light-hearted question. "For heaven's sake, let's get one wedding out of the way before we start talking about another," she laughed. At that moment the telephone rang. Corinne reached over and picked it up. It was

Alicia. "There have been some developments I think you should know about before we all meet up again this evening," she whispered for fear that Chrissy might overhear her, although this was unlikely to happen as she was chilling out in one of the guest suits. "Oh, that sounds ominous," replied Corinne. "No not really, but what I did not have time to tell you when I came back out of the marquee to collect the children was that I'd found Shaun and Jonathan talking to Mark Hammond's partner and what a story she had to tell." Alicia quickly related all that had transpired. "I'm telling you now while she's upstairs, but I think perhaps you should call Laura and Ben and put them in the picture," she suggested. "That certainly is all a big surprise," said Michael, after Corinne had finished talking to them.

By the time Alicia and Chrissy returned to Little Oreford, having left the children with a trusted child minder, the marquee had been transformed into an evening party venue with a dance floor, a substantially restocked free bar and a cold buffet table piled high with tasty sweet and savoury dishes.

There was no doubt about it, Dr Albert Flavell had kept his promise that absolutely no expense was to be spared when it came to his only daughter's big day. 'This wedding must have set your father back at least

£30,000, so just think what we could have done with all that money,' Luke was tempted to say to his bride. But what was the point because he knew she felt the same way too. Entering the marquee, Alicia and Chrissy immediately spotted Corinne and Laura, who'd quickly got to their feet and were waving them over. Chrissy stood back hesitantly as Alicia went around the table embracing Corinne and Michael and Laura and Ben, followed by Jonathan and Shaun, who'd arrived moments ahead of them. "And this is Chrissy Morales," Alicia said, standing aside to introduce their unexpected guest to Corinne and Michael and Laura and Ben. Everyone said they were delighted she could join them and made her feel welcome, but the moment Chrissy set eyes on Corinne and then glanced across at Jonathan, her memory cleared like the sun coming out from behind a cloud. Now she was instantly back with her former boss beside the pool at San Jose's Alhambra Hotel advising them to fly home as soon as they could rather than continue being a source of interest to the shady Jimarenal Corporation.

This had to be the most unusual day of her entire life. so when should she reveal her true identity to Jonathan, whom she could tell was more than a little interested in her? Before she could think any more about it, their

party was being joined by two other guests, who were introduced to her as Laura's daughter Lottie and her husband Andy, the Oreford Inn's Executive Chef.
The marquee was now crowded and noisy with Laura and Ben, back on their feet with Luke, Roxanne and her father to welcome their evening only guests. Seated close by, Heather and Hannah, in full party mode, because they certainly knew how to party, had just been joined by Bob and Annie, whose 'bump' was now beginning to show. Then everyone was on their feet to watch Luke and Roxanne take to the floor for their traditional first dance, and it wasn't many minutes before Shaun had taken Alicia by the hand and was leading her out to dance. "Shall we," invited Jonathan, looking across at Chrissy, who needed little prompting. "We're not going to be left on our own, are we?" said Michael to Corinne, while also getting to his feet. "And I hope that come tomorrow, you'll be wearing your ring announcing our engagement to the whole wide world."
By the end of that never to be forgotten evening, Jonathan and Chrissy had joined Shaun and Alicia in becoming a foursome, fuelled by far more booze than was good for them. When it eventually came to going home, it was simply taken for granted that Jonathan and Chrissy would be sharing Alicia and Shaun's pre-booked

People Carrier. Taking advantage of the covering darkness, both couples embraced and kissed and when they got back to Alicia's, just after midnight and the child minder had been sent on her way, it was only a matter of minutes before they had all said goodnight. For Jonathan and Chrissy, it was a refreshingly new, tender and completely unanticipated experience and they took their time. But for Alicia and Shaun, their hungry love-making was the result of four long years of unrequited passion.

By the time it was all finally spent, Shaun had resolved that if moving to the UK was the price of Alicia's hand, then it was one, he was willingly prepared to pay, and he told her so in whispers as the autumnal dawn light filtered through her bedroom curtains. "Oh Shaun, you can't know just how happy you have made me and, that being the case, I have a treasured gift to share with you, but it will have to wait until a little later," she told him.

Across the hall in the guest suite, Jonathan and Chrissy, wearing the complimentary guest robes provided by their host, were sitting in armchairs on opposite sides of a large picture window and quietly gazing out across the wooded hillside towards Royston's beloved lookout. Jonathan had earlier located the tea making facilities and they were nursing mugs of an English breakfast brew that Chrissy, who only ever drank Costa Rican medium roast coffee, thought was definitely an acquired taste. So, was this the time to reveal her true identity before the situation developed any further? she asked herself and the answer she decided was yes. She rose and casually collected her clutch bag from on top of her clothing that had now been gathered up from its former hurriedly abandoned heap on the floor and carefully laid out on her side of the bed,

"Jonathan, you know you said soon after we were first introduced, that you felt sure we'd met somewhere before; well, I did not take that as a chat-up line because I felt the same way too. Then, when I was introduced to Corinne last night, I suddenly realised where and when we had met, so here's a clue that should jog your memory," she said, producing her Costa Rican crime operative's identity badge and placing it into his hand. Jonathan peered down at it for just a few seconds and then instantly made the connection because when she'd casually mentioned earlier that she was from Costa Rica he'd, immediately thought back to his time there with Corinne. Had it simply have been a memorable holiday, he would have told her all about it because it would have been something they shared in common, but as it had been an experience he'd rather forget, he'd not pursued it. But now, holding the badge in the palm of his hand and staring down at her face, he was right back there again, sitting by that hotel pool and being told quite bluntly by Chrissy and her boss that the pair of them were in danger.

"My God this is amazing!" he uttered. "Honestly Chrissy, I'm finding this quite impossible to believe. So you must help me out by telling me just how you came to leave Costa Rica and get mixed up with Mark Hammond," said Jonathan. "Yes, but you will also have to help me out too because the last my boss and I heard from you and Corinne was when you were abducted on your way to the airport and we feared the worst," she replied.

It did not take many minutes for the two of them to fill in the missing back story pieces of the Jigsaw that had now so symbolically locked their lives together. "So what are we going to do about it all now?" Jonathan asked.

Chrissy thought about this for a few moments. "I seem to have two choices, either to fly back home or to continue the world tour I am thinking of having by coming back with you to Toronto, if you are willing to put me up for a few weeks that is." Downstairs in the large beautifully modernised Victorian kitchen another strand to the story was reaching its climax.

While Anthony was yet again up in his bedroom gaming over the Internet with his best friend Michael, Corina now almost too big for her highchair was sitting at the end of the table between Alicia and Shaun and amazingly, listening intently while he read her a story from her favourite book. It was then that Alicia decided she could not keep her secret from him a moment longer. "You know I said earlier I had a precious gift to share with you, well I think it's high time I told you that Corina is your love child and was never Royston's." It took a few moments for Shaun to internalise those few simple, but totally life-changing words.

"So, at last I have a precious family of my own," he said, tears beginning to well up behind his eyes as he put the story book down and came around to embrace Alicia. There was a vivid picture of a rainbow on the cover. "I think I can truly say I've found the treasure at the end of my rainbow," he said as Corina, oblivious to what was going on, picked up the book and pretended to read it."

The Epilogue

Shaun, without a moment's hesitation, kept his word and came to live with Alicia because after all, in the new world of the Internet, he could make a living where ever he was on the planet. Having a stepfather took Anthony a little while to get used to, but when he saw just how happy his beloved mum now was, he quickly warmed to Shaun. Chrissy flew back to Toronto, so say for a holiday with Jonathan, but never left.

It did not take Mark Hammond long to discover that Chrissy had taken her passport and valuables with her and had probably no intention of returning to The Manders. This was confirmed when he called Laura Jameson, only to be told that she was last seen sharing a ride back to London with one of the guests, which was partly true. Mark purposely made no mention of his recklessly promised £36,000 and Laura now felt too embarrassed to mention it, but she did have another idea.

The following day, Mark was contacted by Jackie at the Gazette saying the Rev Clark had called to tell her how St Michael's, Little Oreford, was going to be saved from closure by his most generous donation so was it OK to put the story in the paper?

Now so neatly caught between the proverbial rock and a hard place, his answer could only be yes.

THE END

NEXT: Read Albany House – Part Five: Looking For Anna

Printed in Great Britain
by Amazon